ST

Commonplace

Commonplace

Christina Rossetti

ET REMOTISSIMA PROPE

Hesperus Classics

Hesperus Classics
Published by Hesperus Press Limited
4 Rickett Street, London SW6 1RU
www.hesperuspress.com

Commonplace first published in 1870
First published by Hesperus Press Limited, 2005
Foreword © Andrew Motion, 2005

Designed and typeset by Fraser Muggeridge
Printed in Jordan by Jordan National Press

ISBN: 1-84391-119-1

CONTENTS

FOREWORD

Christina Rossetti liked to create the impression that she had a secret, perhaps because she was a naturally self-revealing writer. It was her way of keeping something back, of guarding herself while giving so much away. One of her best and best-known poems, 'Goblin Market', is a case in point: the sinuous couplets overflow with suggestions about appetite and its dangers, but they keep us guessing – in the same way that her love-lyrics also throw a veil over the narrative that impels them. Did she love and lose someone, and if so, how? Biographers have given various opinions, but uncertainty lingers. It is essential to the method and the atmosphere of her work; she is a haunted writer as well as a haunting one.

The same is true of her long short story 'Commonplace', which she wrote some time between 1852 and 1870, and was first published with other pieces of short fiction by F.S. Ellis, who also published her brother Dante Gabriel. Although it lacks the sensuality of her best poems, as well as the plangent beauty of her characteristic music, it resembles the rest of her work in being at once definite and withheld. This isn't to say it's interested in mystery as such – rather that its actions are dealt with very quickly and their consequences treated at much greater length. Rossetti is more interested in mood than event: when a boat sinks, we don't see it happen; when a woman has a daughter, we hear next to nothing about the pregnancy; when a man dies, it's over in a sentence. Furthermore, she doesn't identify herself with a particular character, but refracts herself through several, and so confirms a sense of puzzlement in the reader. We finish the story feeling that its clear utterances are less significant than their implications.

Which is as well, considering how often and how badly Rossetti's engine stutters as she tries to drive her characters forward: 'On the morning when our story commences', she says, or 'Forty years before the commencement of this story', or 'The last chapter was parenthetical, this takes up the broken thread of the story'. These are not the remarks of a proto-modernist, drawing our attention to the idea of fiction as a construct; they are simply awkwardnesses, which show a lyric poet grappling with the unfamiliar demands of a prose narrative.

And there are other problems too: occasionally the shape and pace of the story is damaged by an unjustified surge of description; at other times it sounds perfunctory where it means to be allusive.

Yet these imperfections are insignificant compared to the seriousness of Rossetti's achievement. The three central characters – the sisters Catherine, Lucy and Jane Charlmont – are a means of exploring the plight of mid-nineteenth-century middle-class women as they swirl down the marriage-stream towards the rapids of lonely old age. Catherine has promised her dying mother 'to stay here [at their childhood home in Brompton-on-Sea] ready for your father' – who has previously vanished in a boating accident – thereby condemning herself to a fate of 'self-postponement'. Lucy has been disappointed in love and still feels so wounded she can't face visiting London with her sisters, because it will mean having to meet the man in question – Mr Hartley – who is now married to another woman. And the youngest, Jane, is determined to have money at all costs, even if it means attaching herself to the crassly vain Mr Durham of Orpingham Place.

Jane's single-minded pursuit of her goal is condemned by her sisters, who think it venal and sad, but there are hints that Rossetti thinks desperate situations require desperate remedies: Jane's marriage is arid, though not actually appalling. The other two girls look likely to go unrewarded for their finer feelings: Lucy only escapes at the last minute, saved by the sincere but passionless love of Mr Tresham, and Catherine finally accepts that her happiness will come on this earth. 'My dear,' she tells Lucy in the closing lines of the story, 'my future seems further off than yours; but I certainly have a future, and I can wait.' Rossetti is not giving her casting vote to the pious life here; she knows it has its rewards, but she also understands the sacrifices involved.

In her other short prose fiction, Rossetti explored similar and related themes – in 'The Lost Titian' we find her imagining the loss, perhaps irrevocable, of Titian's greatest masterpiece; in 'Vanna's Twins' she examines the stoic devotion of a woman toward the twins of her landlord and lady; in 'Pros and Cons' a rector and his parishioners debate the abolition of pews from their church; and in 'The Waves of This Troublesome World', Rossetti describes the journey of a woman from her childhood, through a disapproved marriage to a Methodist, back to the church and place of her birth, and contentment.

The balance of sympathies in 'Commonplace' is reinforced everywhere: Lucy grows to like the woman now married to the man she loved, and even Jane's husband, the ghastly Mr Durham, realises that he is 'inferior' to the Charlmont sisters. In other words, Rossetti squeezes a doctrine of forgiveness and mutual understanding through the veins of her story, and is generally at pains not to leave her characters feeling antagonistic to one another. But lest this should make 'Commonplace' seem sentimental, she is also at pains to show that the linked problems of love and age are ubiquitous. The difficulties faced by the three sisters are mirrored in all the minor players. The sisters' one-time governess Miss Drum, for instance, who is 'mainly describable by negatives', yet capable of seeing that women must 'do one thing or do the other', on the sole condition that they 'do not become ridiculous'. Whatever their ages, social positions, characters and beliefs, Rossetti's women are all touched by the desperation that Lucy expresses in Chapter 7, and which opens the heart of the book:

'It is easy to ridicule a woman nearly thirty years old for fancying herself beloved without a word said, and suffering deeply under disappointment; yet Lucy Charlmont was no contemptible person... Alone in her own room she might suffer visibly and keenly, but with any eye upon her she would not give way. Sometimes it felt as if the next moment the strain on her nerves might wax unendurable; but such a next moment never came, and she endured still. Only, who is there strong enough, day after day, to strain strength to the utmost, and yet give no sign?'

In this passage we hear the same note that strikes again and again in Rossetti's poems: melancholy and wretchedness, mingled with stoicism. And as her title makes plain, she knew it was a commonplace problem for women in her time. It is her sense of this pain and its pervasiveness that gives the story such raw power. What makes that power twist into our memories is the suggestion that even a money-fixated marriage like Jane's, or a cautious courtship like Lucy's (in which the only 'romantic moment' comes when her fiancé jumps onto the carriage-step of a train as it steams her away from him), is preferable to the singleness of Catherine. From a writer as eagle-eyed about heavenly rewards as Rossetti, this is a remarkable and deeply touching compromise.

– Andrew Motion, 2005

Commonplace

Brompton-on-Sea – any name not in Bradshaw[1] will do – Brompton-on-Sea in April.

The air keen and sunny; the sea blue and rippling, not rolling; everything green, in sight and out of sight, coming on merrily. Birds active over straws and fluff; a hardy butterfly abroad for a change; a second hardy butterfly dancing through mid-air, in and out, and round about the first. A row of houses all alike stands facing the sea – all alike so far as stucco fronts and symmetrical doors and windows could make them so: but one house in the monotonous row was worth looking at, for the sake of more numerous hyacinths and early roses in its slip of front garden, and on several of its window sills. Judging by appearances, and for once judging rightly, this must be a private residence on an esplanade full of lodging houses.

A pretty house inside too, snug in winter, fresh in summer; now in mid-spring sunny enough for an open window, and cool enough for a bright fire in the breakfast room.

Three ladies sat at the breakfast table, three maiden ladies, obviously sisters by strong family likeness, yet with individual differences strong also. The eldest, Catherine, Miss Charlmont, having entered her thirty-third year, had taken on all occasions to appearing in some sort of cap. She began the custom at thirty, when also she gave up dancing, and adopted lace over her neck and arms in evening dress. Her manner was formal and kindly, savouring of the provinces rather than of the capital; but of the provinces in their towns, not in their old country seats. Yet she was a well-bred gentlewoman in all essentials, tall and fair, a handsome member of a handsome family. She presided over the tea and coffee, and despite modern usage retained a tea tray.

Opposite her sat Lucy, less striking in features and complexion, but with an expression of quicker sensibility. Rather pretty and very sweet-looking, not turned thirty as yet, and on some points treated by Catherine as still a young thing. She had charge of the loaf and ham, and like her elder sister never indulged in opening letters till everyone at table had been served.

The third, Jane, free of meat-and-drink responsibilities, opened letters or turned over the newspaper as she pleased. She was youngest by many years, and came near to being very beautiful. Her profile was almost Grecian, her eyes were large, and her fair hair grew in wavy abundance. At first sight she threw Catherine and Lucy completely into the shade; afterwards, in spite of their additional years, they sometimes were preferred, for her face only of the three could be thought insipid. Pleasure and displeasure readily showed themselves in it, but the pleasure would be frivolous and the displeasure often unreasonable. A man might fall in love with Jane, but no one could make a friend of her; Catherine and Lucy were sure to have friends, however they might lack lovers.

On the morning when our story commences, the elders were busied with their respective charges, whilst Jane already sipped her tea and glanced up and down the Births, Marriages and Deaths, in the *Times Supplement*. There she sat, with one elbow on the table and her long lashes showing to advantage over downcast eyes. Dress was with her a matter for deep study, and her pink-and-white breakfast suit looked as fresh and blooming as April's self. Her hair fell long and loose over her shoulders, in becoming freedom; and Catherine, gazing at her, felt a motherly pride in the pretty creature to whom, for years, she had performed a mother's duty; and Lucy felt how young and fresh Jane was, and remembered that she herself was turned twenty-nine: but if the thought implied regret it was untinctured by envy.

Jane read aloud: ' "Halbert to Jane" – I wish I were Jane. And here, positively, are two more Janes, and not me. "Catherine" – that's a death. Lucy, I don't see you anywhere. Catherine was eighty-nine, and much respected. "Mrs Anstruther of a son and heir." I wonder if those are the Anstruthers I met in Scotland: she was very ugly, and short. "Everilda Stella" – how can anybody be Everilda?' Then, with a sudden accession of interest, 'Why, Lucy, Everilda Stella has actually married your Mr Hartley!'

Lucy started, but no one noticed her. Catherine said, 'Don't say "your" Mr Hartley, Jane: that is not a proper way of speaking about a married gentleman to an unmarried lady. Say "the Mr Hartley you know", or, "the Mr Hartley you have met in London". Besides, I am acquainted with him also; and very likely it is a different person. Hartley is not an uncommon name.'

'Oh, but it is that Mr Hartley, sister,' retorted Jane, and she read:

'"On Monday the 13th, at the parish church, Fenton, by the Revd James Durham, uncle of the bride, Alan Hartley, Esq., of the Woodlands, Gloucestershire, to Everilda Stella, only child and presumptive heiress of George Durham, Esq., of Orpingham Place, in the same county."'

2

Forty years before the commencement of this story, William Charlmont, an Indian army surgeon, penniless, except for his pay, had come unexpectedly into some hundreds a year, left him by a maiden great-aunt, who had seen him but once – and that when he was five years old, on which occasion she boxed his ears for misspelling 'elephant'. His stoicism under punishment – for he neither roared nor whined – may have won her heart; at any rate, from whatever motive, she, years afterwards, disappointed three nephews and a female first cousin by leaving every penny she was worth to him. This moderate accession of fortune justified him in consulting both health and inclination by exchanging regimental practice in India for general practice in England: and a combination of apparently trifling circumstances led him, soon after his return home, to settle at the then infant watering place of Brompton-on-Sea, of which the reputation had just been made by a royal duke's visit; and the tide of fashion was setting to its shore.

The house in which our story opens then stood alone, and belonged to a clergyman's widow. As she possessed, besides, an only daughter, and but a small life annuity – nothing more – she sought for a lodger, and was glad to find one in the new medical practitioner. The widow, Mrs Turner, was – and felt herself to be – no less a gentlewoman when she let lodgings than when with her husband and child she had occupied the same house alone; no less so when after breakfast she donned a holland apron and helped Martha, the maid, to make Mr Charlmont's bed, than when in old days she had devoted her mornings to visiting and relieving her poorer neighbours.

Her daughter, Kate, felt their altered fortunes more painfully, and showed, sometimes by uncomfortable bashfulness, sometimes by anxious self-assertion, how much importance she attached to the verdict of Mrs Grundy.[2] Her mother's holland apron was to her a daily humiliation, and single-handed Martha an irritating shortcoming. She chilled old friends by declining invitations, because her wardrobe lacked variety, and shunned new acquaintances lest they should call at some moment when herself or her mother might have to answer the door. A continual aim at false appearances made her constrained and affected; and persons who would never have dwelt upon the fact that Mrs Turner let lodgings, were certain to have it recalled to mind by Miss Turner's uneasiness.

But Kate owned a pretty face, adorned by a pink-and-white complexion, most refreshing to eyes that had ached under an Indian sun. At first Mr Charlmont set her down as merely affected and silly; then he began to dwell on the fact that, however silly and affected, she was indisputably pretty; next he reflected that reverses of fortune deserve pity and demand every gentleman's most courteous consideration. In himself such consideration at once took the form of books lent from his library; of flowers for the drawing room, and fruit for dessert. Kate, to do her justice, was no flirt, and saw without seeing his attentions; but her more experienced mother seeing, pondered and seized – or made – an opportunity for checking her lodger's intimacy. Mr Charlmont, however, was not to be rebuffed; opposition made him earnest, whilst the necessity of expressing his feelings gave them definiteness: and not many months later Kate, with the house for her dowry, became Mrs William Charlmont; the obnoxious lodger developed into an attached and dear husband, and Mrs Turner retired on the life annuity to finish her days in independence.

A few years passed in hopes and disappointments. When hope had dwindled to despondency, a little girl came – Catherine; after another few years a second girl, named Lucy in memory of her grandmother Turner, who had not lived to see her namesake. Then more years passed without a baby; and in due course the sisters were sent to Miss Drum's school as day-boarders, their mother having become ailing and indolent.

Time went on, and the girls grew wiser and prettier – Catherine very pretty. When she was nearly twelve years old, Mr Charlmont said one evening to his wife, 'I have made my will, Kate, and left everything to you in the first instance, and between the children after you.' And she answered, blushing – she was still comely, and a blush became her: 'Oh, William, but suppose another baby should come?' 'Well, I should make my will over again,' he replied: but he did not guess why his wife blushed and spoke eagerly; he had quite given up such hopes.

Mr Charlmont was fond of boating, and one day, when the girls were at home for the Easter holidays, he offered to take them both for a row; but Catherine had a bad cold, and as Lucy was not a good sailor he did not care to take charge of her without her sister. His wife never had liked boating. Thus it was that he went alone. The morning was dull and chilly; but there was no wind, and the sea was almost smooth. He took dinner and fishing tackle in the boat with him, and gave notice that he should not be at home till the evening.

No wind, no sun; the day grew duller and duller, dimmer and dimmer. A smokelike fog, beginning on land, spread from the cliffs to the beach, from the beach over the water's edge; further and further it spread, beyond sight – it might be for miles over the sea. No wind blew to shift the dense fog which hid seamarks and landmarks alike. As day waned towards evening and darkness deepened, all the fisherfolk gathered on the beach in pain and fear for those at sea. They lit a bonfire, they shouted, they fired off an old gun or two, such as they could get together, and still they watched, and feared, and hoped. Now one boat came in, now another; some guided by the glare, some by the sound of the firing: at last, by midnight, every boat had come in safe, except Mr Charlmont's.

As concerned him, that night was only like all nights and all days afterwards; for neither man, nor boat, nor waif, nor stray from either, ever drifted ashore.

Mrs Charlmont took the news of her husband's disappearance very quietly indeed. She did not cry or fret, or propose any measures for finding him; but she bade Catherine be sure to have tea ready when he came in. This she repeated every day, and often in the day; and would herself sit by a window looking out towards the sea, smiling and cheerful. If anyone spoke to her, she would answer at random, but quite cheerfully. She rose or went to bed when her old nurse called her, she ate and drank when food was set before her; but she originated nothing, and seemed indifferent to everything except the one anxiety: that tea should be ready for her husband on his return.

The holidays over, Lucy went back to Miss Drum's, trudging to and fro daily; but Catherine stayed at home to keep house and sit with her poor dazed mother.

A few months and the end came. One night, nurse insisted with unusual determination on the girls going to bed early; but before daybreak Catherine was roused out of her sleep to see a new little sister and her dying mother.

Life was almost gone, and with the approach of death a sort of consciousness had returned. Mrs Charlmont looked hard at Catherine, who was crying bitterly, and taking her hand said distinctly: 'Catherine, promise to stay here ready for your father when he comes on shore – promise some of you to stay here: don't let him come on shore and find me gone and no one – don't let the body come on shore and find us all gone and no one – promise me, Catherine!'

And Catherine promised.

* * *

Mr Charlmont died a wealthy man. He had enjoyed a large lucrative practice, and had invested his savings profitably: by his will, and on their mother's death, an ample provision remained for his daughters. Strictly speaking, it remained for Catherine and Lucy: the baby, Jane, was unavoidably left dependent on her sisters; but on sisters who, in afterlife, never felt that their own right to their father's property was more obvious or more valid than hers.

Mr Charlmont had appointed but one trustee for his daughters – Mr Drum, only brother of their schoolmistress, a thoroughly honest lawyer, practising and thriving in Brompton-on-Sea; a man somewhat younger than himself, who had speculated adroitly both with him and for him. On Mrs Charlmont's death, Mr Drum proposed sending the two elder girls to a fashionable boarding school near London, and letting nurse, with a wet nurse under her, keep house in the old home with baby: but

Catherine set her face against this plan, urging her promise to her dying mother as a reason for not going away; and so held to her point that Mr Drum yielded, and agreed that the girls, who could not bear to be parted, should continue on the same terms as before at his sister's school. Miss Drum, an intimate friend of their mother's, engaged to take them into such suitable society as might offer until Catherine should come of age; and as she resided within two minutes' walk of their house, this presented no difficulty. At twenty-one, under their peculiar circumstances, Catherine was to be considered old enough to chaperone her sisters. Nurse, a respectable elderly woman, was to remain as housekeeper and personal attendant on the children; and a wet nurse, to be succeeded by a nursery-girl, with two other maids, completed the household.

Catherine, though only in her thirteenth year, already looked grave, staid and tall enough for a girl of sixteen when these arrangements were entered into. The sense of responsibility waxed strong within her, and with the motherly position came something of the motherly instinct of self-postponement to her children.

3

The last chapter was parenthetical, this takes up the broken thread of the story.

Breakfast over, and her sisters gone their several ways, Lucy Charlmont seized the *Times Supplement* and read the Hartley-Durham paragraph over to herself: – 'On Monday the 13th, at the parish church, Fenton, by the Revd James Durham, uncle of the bride, Alan Hartley, Esq., of the Woodlands, Gloucestershire, to Everilda Stella, only child and presumptive heiress of George Durham, Esq., of Orpingham Place, in the same county.'

There remained no lurking-place for doubt. Mr Hartley – 'her' Mr Hartley, as Jane dubbed him – had married Everilda Stella, a presumptive heiress. Thus concluded Lucy's one romance.

Poor Lucy! The romance had been no fault of hers, perhaps not even a folly: it had arisen thus. When Miss Charlmont was twenty-one, Lucy was eighteen, and had formally come out under her sister's wing; thenceforward going with her to balls and parties from time to time, and staying with her at friends' houses in town or country. This paying visits had entailed the necessity of Jane's having a governess. Miss Drum had by that time 'relinquished tuition', as she herself phrased it, and retired on a comfortable competence earned by her own exertions; therefore, to Miss Drum's school Jane could not go. Lucy, when the subject was started, declared with affectionate impulsiveness that she would not pay visits at all, or else that she and Catherine might pay them separately; but Catherine, who considered herself in the place of mother to both her sisters, and whose standard of justice to both alike was inflexible, answered, 'My dear' – when Miss Charlmont said 'my dear' it ended a discussion – 'My dear, Jane must have a governess. She shall always be with us in the holidays, and shall leave the schoolroom for good when she is eighteen, and old enough to enter society; but at present I must think of you and your prospects.' So Jane had a fashionable governess, fresh from a titled family, and versed in accomplishments and the art of dress, whilst Catherine commenced her duties as chaperone. Lucy thought that her sister, handsomer than herself and not much older, might have prospects too, and tried hard to discover chances for her; but Catherine nursed no such fancies on her own account. Her promise to her dying mother that some one of them should always be on the spot at Brompton-on-Sea – literally meant at the moment – she resolved as literally to fulfil, even whilst she felt that only by one not fully in her right mind could such a promise have been exacted. Grave and formal in manner, dignified in person, and in disposition reserved, though amiable, she never seemed to notice or to return attentions paid her by any man of her acquaintance; and if one of these ever committed himself so far as to hazard an offer, she kept his secret and her own.

Lucy, meanwhile, indulged on her own account the usual hopes and fears of a young woman. At first, all parties and visits were delightful, one not much less so than another; then a difference made itself felt between them: some parties turned out dull, and some visits tedious. The last year of Lucy's going everywhere with Catherine – before, that is, she began dividing engagements with Jane (for until Lucy should be turned thirty, self-chaperoning was an inadmissable enormity in Miss Charlmont's eyes, in spite of what she had herself done: as she said, her own had been an exceptional case) – in that last year the two sisters had together spent a month with Dr Tyke, whose wife had been before marriage another Lucy Charlmont, and a favourite cousin of their father's: concerning her, tradition even hinted that, in bygone years, she had refused the penniless army surgeon.

Be this as it may, at Mrs Tyke's house in London the sisters spent one certain June, and then and there Lucy 'met her fate', as with a touch of sentiment, bordering on sentimentality, she recorded in her diary one momentous first meeting. Alan Hartley was a nephew of Dr Tyke's – handsome and clever on the surface, if not deep within. He had just succeeded his father at the Woodlands, had plenty of money, no profession, and no hindrance to idling away any amount of time with any pretty woman who was pleasant company. Such a woman was Lucy Charlmont. He harboured no present thoughts of marriage, but she did; he really did pay just as much attention to a dozen girls elsewhere, but she judged by his manner to herself, and drew from it a false conclusion. That delightful June came to an end, and he had not spoken; but two years later occurred a second visit, as pleasant and as full of misunderstanding as the first. Meanwhile, she had refused more than one offer. Poor Lucy Charlmont: her folly, even if it was folly, had not been very blameable.

The disenchantment came no less painfully than unexpectedly: and Lucy, ready to cry, but ashamed of crying for such a cause, thrust the *Supplement* out of sight and, sitting down, forced herself to face the inevitable future. One thing was certain: she could not meet Alan – in her thoughts he had long been Alan, and now it cost her an effort of recollection to stiffen him back into Mr Hartley – she must not meet Mr Hartley till she could reckon on seeing him and his wife with friendly composure. Oh! why – why – why had she all along misunderstood him, and he never understood her? Not to meet him, it would be necessary to decline the invitation from Mrs Tyke, which she had looked forward to and longed for during weeks past, and which, in the impartial judgement of Miss Charlmont, it was her turn, not Jane's, to accept; which, moreover, might arrive by any post. Jane she knew would be ready enough to pay a visit out of turn, but Catherine would want a reason; and what reason could she give? On one point, however, she was determined: that, with or without her reasons being accepted as reasonable, go she would not. Then came the recollection of a cracker she had pulled with him, and kept in her pocketbook ever since; and of a card he had left for her and her sister – or, as she had fondly fancied, mainly for herself – before the last return from Mrs Tyke's to Brompton-on-Sea. Treasures no longer to be treasured, despoiled treasures – she denied herself the luxury of a sigh, as she thrust them between the bars of the grate and watched them burn.

4

'Lucy, Jane,' said Miss Charlmont, some days afterwards, addressing her sisters and holding up an open letter – 'Mrs Tyke has sent a very kind invitation, asking me, with one of you, to stay a month at her house, and to fix the day. It is your turn, Lucy; so, if you have no objection, I shall write, naming next Thursday for our journey to London. Jane, I shall ask Miss Drum to stay with you during our absence; I think she will be all the better for a change, and there is no person more fit to have the charge of you. So don't be dull, dear, till we come back.'

But Jane pouted, and said in a cross tone, 'Really, sister, you need not settle everything now for me, as if I were a baby. I don't want Miss Drum, who is as old as the hills and as solemn. Can't you write to Mrs Tyke and say that I cannot be left alone here? What difference could it make in her large house?'

For once Catherine answered her favourite sister with severity, 'Jane, you know why it is impossible for us all to leave home together. This is the last year you will be called upon to remain behind, for after Lucy's next birthday it is agreed between us that she will take turns with me in chaperoning you. Do not make what may be our last excursion together unpleasant by your unkindness.'

Still Jane was not silenced. 'At any rate, it need not be Miss Drum. I will stay here alone, or I will have somebody more amusing than Miss Drum.'

Before Catherine could reply, Lucy with an effort struck into the dispute. 'Jane, don't speak like that to our sister; I should be ashamed to speak to her so. Still, Catherine,' she continued, without noticing a muttered retort from the other, 'after all, I am going to side with Jane on the main point, and ask you to take her to Notting Hill, and leave me at home to keep house with dear old Miss Drum. This really was my own wish before Jane spoke, so pray let us not say another word on the subject.'

But Catherine saw how pale and languid she looked, and stood firm. 'No, Lucy, that would be unreasonable; Jane ought not to have made any difficulty. You have lost your colour lately and your appetite, and need a change more than either of us. I shall write to Mrs Tyke, promising her and the Doctor your company next Thursday; Jane will make up her mind like a good girl, and I am sure you, my dear, will oblige me by not withholding your assent.'

For the first time 'my dear' did not close the debate. 'Catherine,' said Lucy earnestly, whilst, do what she would, tears gathered in her eyes, 'I am certain you will not press me further when I assure you that I do not feel equal to paying this visit. I have felt weak lately,' she went on hurriedly, 'and I cannot tell you how much I long for the quiet of a month at home rather than in that perpetual bustle. Merely for my own sake, Jane must go.'

Catherine said no more just then; but later, alone with Lucy, resumed the subject so far as to ask whether she continued in the same mind, and answered her flurried 'yes' by no word of remonstrance, but by an affectionate kiss. This was all which passed between them; neither then nor afterwards did the younger sister feel certain whether Catherine had or had not guessed her secret.

Miss Drum was invited to stay with Lucy in her solitude, and gladly accepted the invitation. Lucy was her favourite, and when they were together they petted each other very tenderly.

Jane, having gained her point, recovered her good humour, and lost no time in exposing the deficiencies of her wardrobe. 'Sister,' she said, smiling her prettiest and most coaxing smile, 'you can't think how poor I am, and how few clothes I've got.'

Catherine, trying to appear serenely unconscious of the drift of this speech, replied, 'Let us look over your wardrobe, dear, and we will bring it into order. Lucy will help, I know, and we can have Miss Smith to work here too, if necessary.'

'Oh dear, no!' cried Jane; 'there is no looking over what does not exist. If it comes to furbishing up old tags and rags, here I stay. Why, you're as rich as Jews, you and Lucy, and could give me five pounds apiece without ever missing it; and not so much of a gift either, for I'm sure poor papa would never have left me such a beggar if he had known about me.'

This argument had been used more than once before. Catherine looked hurt. Lucy said, 'You should remember that you have exactly the same allowance for dress and pocket money that we have ourselves, and we both make it do.'

'Of course,' retorted Jane, with latent spitefulness; 'and when I'm as old and wise as you two, I may manage as well; but at present it is different. Besides, if I spend most on dress, you spend most on books and music, and dress is a great deal more amusing. And if I dressed like an old fright, I should like to know who'd look at me. You don't want me to be another old maid, I suppose.'

Lucy flushed up, and tried to keep her temper in silence: her sore point had been touched. Catherine, accustomed in such cases to protest first and yield afterwards, but half ashamed that Lucy's eye should mark the process from beginning to end, drew Jane out of the room, and with scarcely a word more wrote her a cheque for ten pounds, and dropped the subject of looking over her wardrobe.

An hour after the sisters had started for London, Miss Drum arrived to take their place.

Miss Drum was tall in figure, rather slim and well preserved, with pale complexion, hair and eyes, and an unvarying tone of voice. She was mainly describable by negatives. She was neither unladylike, nor clever, nor deficient in education. She was old, but not very infirm; and neither an altogether obsolete nor a youthful dresser, though with some tendency towards the former style. Propriety was the most salient of her attributes, and was just too salient to be perfect. She was not at all amusing; in fact, rather tiresome, with an unflagging intention of being agreeable. From her Catherine acquired a somewhat old-fashioned formality; from her, also, high principles, and the instinct of self-denial. And because unselfishness, itself a negative, was Miss Drum's characteristic virtue, and because her sympathy, however prosy in expression, was sterling in quality, therefore Lucy, sore with unavowed heart-sorrow, could bear her companionship, and run down to welcome her at the door with affectionate cordiality.

5

London Bridge Station, with its whirl of traffic, seems no bad emblem of London itself: vast, confused, busy, orderly, more or less dirty; implying enormous wealth in some quarter or other; providing luxuries for the rich, necessaries for the poor; thronged by rich and poor alike, idle and industrious, young and old, men and women.

London Bridge Station at its cleanest is soiled by thousands of feet passing to and fro: on a drizzling day each foot deposits mud in its passage, takes and gives mud, leaves its impress in mud; on such a day the Station is not attractive to persons fresh from the unfailing cleanliness of sea coast and inland country; and on such a day – when, by the late afternoon, the drizzle had done, and the platform had suffered each its worst – on such a day Miss Charlmont and her pretty sister, fresh and fastidious from sea salt and country sweetness, arrived at the Station.

Dr Tyke's carriage was there to meet the train. Dr Tyke's coachman, footman and horses were fat, as befitted a fat master, whose circumstances and whose temperament might be defined as fat also; for ease, good nature and fat have an obvious affinity.

'Should the hood be up or down?' The rain had ceased, and Miss Charlmont, who always described London as stifling, answered, 'Up.' Jane, leaning back with an elegant ease, which nature had given and art perfected, felt secretly ashamed of Catherine, who sat bolt upright, according to her wont, and would no more have lolled in an open carriage than on the high-backed, scant-seated chair of her schooldays.

The City looked at once dingy and glaring – dingy with unconsumed smoke, and glaring here and there with early-lighted gas. When Waterloo Bridge had been crossed, matters brightened somewhat, and Oxford Street showed not amiss. Along the Edgware Road dirt and dinginess reasserted their sway; but when the carriage finally turned into Notting Hill and drove amongst the crescents, roads and gardens of that cleanly suburb, a winding-up shower, brisk and brief, not drizzly, cleared the way for the sun, and finished off the afternoon with a rainbow.

Dr Tyke's abode was named Apple Trees House, though the orchard whence the name was derived had disappeared before the memory of the oldest inhabitant. The carriage drew up, the door swung open: down the staircase came flying a little, slim woman, with outstretched hands and words of welcome; auburn-haired, though she had outlived the last of the fifties, and cheerful, though the want of children had not ceased to be felt as a hopeless disappointment: a pale-complexioned, high-voiced, little woman – all that remained of that fair cousin Lucy of bygone years and William Charlmont.

Behind her, and more deliberately, descended her husband, elastic of step, rotund of figure, bright-eyed, rosy, white-headed, not altogether unlike a robin redbreast that had been caught in the snow. Mrs Tyke had a habit of running on with long-winded, perfectly harmless commonplaces; but notwithstanding her garrulity, she never uttered an ill-natured word or a false one. Dr Tyke, burdened with an insatiable love of fun and a ready, if not a witty, wit, was addicted to venting jokes, repartees, and so-called anecdotes; the last not always unimpeachably authentic.

Such were the hosts. The house was large and light, with a laboratory for the Doctor, who dabbled in chemistry, and an aviary for his wife, who doted on pets. The walls of the sitting rooms were hung with engravings, not with family portraits, real or sham: in fact, no sham was admitted within doors, unless imaginary anecdotes and quotations must be stigmatised as shams; and as to these, when taxed with invention, the Doctor would only reply by his favourite Italian phrase: '*Se non è vero è ben trovato.*'[3]

* * *

'Jane,' said Mrs Tyke, as the three ladies sat over a late breakfast, the Doctor having already retreated to the laboratory and his newspaper: 'Jane, I think you have made a conquest.'

Jane looked down in silence, with a conscious simper. Catherine spoke rather anxiously: 'Indeed, Cousin Lucy, I have noticed what you allude to, and I have spoken to Jane about not encouraging Mr Durham. He is not at all a man she can really like, and she ought to be most careful not to let herself be misunderstood. Jane, you ought indeed.'

But Jane struck merrily in: 'Mr Durham is old enough and – ahem! – handsome enough to take care of himself, sister. And, besides' – with a touch of mimicry, which recalled his pompous manner – 'Orpingham Place, my dear madam, Orpingham Place is a very fine place, a very fine place indeed. Our pineapples can really hardly be got rid of, and our prize pigs can't see out of their eyes; they can't indeed, my dear young lady, though it's not pretty talk for a pretty young lady to listen to… Very well, if the pines and the pigs are smitten, why shouldn't I marry the pigs and the pines?'

'Why not?' cried Mrs Tyke with a laugh; but Miss Charlmont, looking disturbed, rejoined: 'Why not, certainly, if you like Mr Durham; but do you like Mr Durham? And, whether or not, you ought not to laugh at him.'

Jane pouted: 'Really one would think I was a child still! As to Mr Durham, when he knows his own mind and speaks, you may be quite sure I shall know my own mind and give him his answer… Orpingham Place, my dear Miss Catherine, the finest place in the county; the finest place in three counties, whatever my friend the Duke may say. A charming neighbourhood, Miss Catherine; her Grace the Duchess, the most affable woman you can imagine, and my lady the Marchioness, a fine woman – a very fine woman. But they can't raise such pines as my pines; they can't do it, you know; they haven't the means, you know… Come now, sister, don't look cross; when I'm Mrs Durham, you shall have your slice off the pigs and the pines.'

6

Everilda Stella, poor Lucy's unconscious rival, had married out of the schoolroom. Pretty she was not, but with much piquancy of face and manner, and a talent for private theatricals. These advantages – gilded, perhaps, by her reputation as presumptive heiress – attracted to her a suitor, to whose twenty years' seniority she felt no objection. Mr Hartley wooed and won her in the brief space of an Easter holiday; and bore her, nothing loath, to London, to enjoy the gaieties of the season. Somewhat to the bridegroom's annoyance, Mr Durham accompanied the newly married couple to town, and shared their pretty house in Kensington.

Alan Hartley, a favourite nephew of Dr Tyke, had, as we know, been very intimate at his house in old days. Now he was proud to present his little wife of sixteen to his uncle and aunt, though somewhat mortified at having also to introduce his father-in-law, whose pompous manners and habit of dragging titled personages into his discourse put him to the blush. Alan had dropped Everilda, and called his wife simply Stella; her father dubbed her Pug; Everilda she was named, in accordance with the taste of her peerage-studious mother. This lady was accustomed to describe herself as of a north-country family – a Leigh of the Leazes; which conveyed an old-manorial notion to persons unacquainted with Newcastle-on-Tyne. But this by the way: Mrs Durham had died before the opening of our tale.

At their first visit they were shown into the drawing room by a smiling maidservant, and requested to wait, as Dr and Mrs Tyke were expected home every moment. Stella looked very winning in her smart hat and feather and jaunty jacket, and Alan would have abandoned himself to all the genial glow of a bridegroom, but for Mr Durham's behaviour. That gentleman began by placing his hat on the floor between his feet, and flicking his boots with a crimson silk pocket handkerchief. This done, he commenced a survey of the apartment, accompanied by an apt running comment: 'Hem, no pictures – cheap engravings; a four-and-sixpenny Brussels carpet; a smallish mirror, wants regilding. Pug, my pet, that's a neat antimacassar: see if you can't carry off the stitch in your eye. A piano – a harp; fiddlestick!'

When Dr and Mrs Tyke entered, they found the Hartleys looking uncomfortable and Mr Durham red and pompous after his wont; also, in opening the door, they caught the sound of 'fiddlestick!'. All these symptoms, with the tact of kindness, they ignored. The bride was kissed, the father-in-law taken for granted, and Alan welcomed as if no one in the room had looked guilty.

'Come to lunch and take a hunch,' said the Doctor, offering his arm to Stella. 'Mother Bunch is rhyme, but not reason; you shall munch and I will scrunch – that's both. "Ah! you may well look surprised," as the foreign ambassador admitted when the ancient Britons noticed that he had no tail. But you won't mind when you know us better; I'm no worse than a barrel organ.'

Yet with all Dr Tyke's endeavour to be funny – and this time it cost him an effort – and with all his wife's facile commonplaces, two of the guests seemed ill at ease. Alan felt, as it were with every nerve, the impression his father-in-law must produce, while Stella, less sensitive for herself, was out of countenance for her husband's sake. Mr Durham, indeed, was pompous and unabashed as ever; but whilst he answered commonplace remarks by remarks no less commonplace, he appeared to be, as in fact he was, occupied in scrutinising, and mentally valuing, the plate and china.

'Charming weather,' said Mrs Tyke, with an air of intelligent originality.

'Yes, ma'am; fine weather, indeed; billing and cooing weather; ha! ha!' – with a glance across the table. 'Now I dare say your young ladies know what to do in this weather.'

'We have no children,' and Mrs Tyke whispered, lest her husband should hear. Then, after a pause, 'I dare say Orpingham Place was just coming into beauty when you left.'

Mr Durham thrust his thumbs into his waistcoat pockets and leant back for conversation. 'Well, I don't know what to say to that – I don't indeed; I don't know which the season is when Orpingham Place is *not* in beauty. Its conservatories were quite a local lion last winter – quite a local lion, as my friend the Duke remarked to me; and he said he must bring the Duchess over to see them, and he did bring her Grace over; and I gave them a luncheon in the largest conservatory, such as I don't suppose they sit down to every day. For the nobility have blood, if you please, and the literary beggars are welcome to all the brains they've got' – the Doctor smiled, Alan winced visibly – 'but you'll find it's us city men who've got backbone, and backbone's the best to wear, as I observed to the Duke that very day when I gave him such a glass of port as he hasn't got in his cellar. I said it to him, just as I say it to you, ma'am, and he didn't contradict me; in fact, you know, he couldn't.'

After this it might have been difficult to start conversation afresh – when, happily, Jane entered, late for luncheon, and with an apology for her sister, who was detained elsewhere. She went through the necessary introductions, and took her seat between Dr Tyke and Mr Durham, thus commanding an advantageous view of the bride, whom she mentally set down as nothing particular in any way.

Alan had never met Jane before. He asked her after Miss Charlmont and Lucy – after Lucy especially, who was 'a very charming old friend' of his, as he explained to Stella. For some minutes Mr Durham sat silent, much impressed by Jane's beauty and grace; this gave people breathing-time for the recovery of ease and good humour; and it was not till Dr Tyke had uttered three successive jokes, and everyone, except Mr Durham, had laughed at them, that the master of Orpingham Place could think of any remark worthy of his attractive neighbour; and then, with much originality, he too observed: '…Charming weather, Miss Jane.'

And Jane answered with a smile; for was not this the widower of Orpingham Place?

That Mr Durham's conversation on subsequent occasions gained in range of subject is clear from Jane's quotations in the last chapter. And that Mr Durham was alive to Jane's fascinations appeared pretty evident, as he not only called frequently at Apple Trees House, but made up parties, to which Dr and Mrs Tyke, and the Miss Charlmonts, were invariably asked.

7

Gaiety in London, sadness by the sea.

Lucy did her very best to entertain Miss Drum with the cheerfulness of former visits; in none of which had she shown herself more considerate of the old lady's tastes than now. She made breakfast half an hour earlier than usual; she culled for her interesting scraps from the newspaper; she gave her an arm up and down the esplanade on sunny days; she reclaimed the most unpromising strayed stitches in her knitting; she sang her old-fashioned favourite ballads for an hour or so before teatime, and after tea till bedtime played energetically at backgammon: yet Miss Drum was sensible of a change. All Lucy's efforts could not make her cheeks rosy and plump and her laugh spontaneous; could not make her step elastic or her eyes bright.

It is easy to ridicule a woman nearly thirty years old for fancying herself beloved without a word said, and suffering deeply under disappointment: yet Lucy Charlmont was no contemptible person. However at one time deluded, she had never let a hint of her false hopes reach Mr Hartley's observation; and however now dis-appointed, she fought bravely against a betrayal of her plight. Alone in her own room she might suffer visibly and keenly, but with any eye upon her she would not give way. Sometimes it felt as if the next moment the strain on her nerves might wax unendurable; but such a next moment never came, and she endured still. Only, who is there strong enough, day after day, to strain strength to the utmost, and yet give no sign?

'My dear,' said Miss Drum, contemplating Lucy over her spectacles and across the backgammon board one evening, when the eyes looked more sunken than ever and the whole face more haggard, 'I am sure you do not take exercise enough. You really must do more than give me an arm on the esplanade; all your bloom is gone, and you are much too thin. Promise me that you will take at least one long walk in the day whenever the weather is not unfavourable.'

Lucy stroked her old friend's hand fondly: 'I will take walks when my sisters are at home again; but I have not you here always.'

Miss Drum insisted: 'Do not say so, my dear, or I shall feel bound to go home again; and that I should not like at all, as we both know. Pray oblige me by promising.'

Thus urged, Lucy promised, and in secret rejoiced that for at least an hour or two of the day she should thenceforward be alone, relieved from the scrutiny of those dim, affectionate eyes. And truly she needed some relief. By day she could forbid her thoughts to shape themselves, even mentally, into words, although no effort could banish the vague, dull sorrow which was all that might now remain to her of remembrance. But by night, when sleep paralysed self-restraint, then her dreams were haunted by distorted spectres of the past; never alluring or endearing – for this she was thankful – but sometimes monstrous, and always impossible to escape from. Night after night she would awake from such dreams, struggling and sobbing, with less and less conscious strength to resume daily warfare.

Soon she allowed no weather to keep her indoors at the hour for walking, and Miss Drum, who was a hardy disciple of the old school, encouraged her activity. She always sought the sea: not the smooth, civilised esplanade, but the rough, irreclaimable shingle; to stray to and fro till the last moment of her freedom; to and fro, to and fro, at once listless and unresting, with wide, absent eyes fixed on the monotonous waves, which they did not see. Gradually a morbid fancy grew upon her that one day she should behold her father's body washed ashore, and that she should know the face: from a waking fancy, this began to haunt her dreams with images unutterably loathsome. Then she walked no more on the shingle, but took to wandering along green lanes and country roads.

But no one struggling persistently against weakness fails to overcome: also, however prosaic the statement may sound, air and exercise *will* take effect on persons of sound constitution. Something of Lucy's lost colour showed itself, by fits and starts at first, next steadily; her appetite came back, however vexed she might feel at its return; at last fatigue brought sounder sleep, and the hollow eyes grew less sunken. This refreshing sleep was the turning point in her case; it supplied strength for the day, whilst each day in its turn brought with it fewer and fewer demands upon her strength. Seven weeks after Miss Drum exacted the promise, Lucy, though graver of aspect, and at heart sadder than before Alan Hartley's wedding, had recovered in a measure her look of health and her interest in the details of daily life. She no longer greatly dreaded meeting her sisters when at length their much-prolonged absence should terminate; and in spite of some nervousness in the anticipation, felt confident that even a sight of Mr and Mrs Hartley would not upset the outward composure of her decorum.

Miss Drum triumphed in the success of her prescription, and brought forward parallel instances within her own experience. 'That is right,' she would say, 'my dear; take another slice of the mutton where it is not overdone. There is nothing like exercise for giving an appetite, only the mutton should not be overdone. You cannot remember Sarah Smith, who was with me before your dear mother entrusted you to my care; but I assure you three doctors had given her over as a confirmed invalid when I prescribed for her,' and the old lady laughed gently at her own wit. 'I made her take a walk every day, let the weather be what it might; and gave her nice, juicy mutton to eat, with a change to beef, or a chicken, now and then for variety; and very soon you would not have known her for the same girl; and Dr Grey remarked, in his funny way, that I ought to be an M.D. myself.' Or, again: 'Lucy, my dear, you recollect my French assistant, Mademoiselle Leclerc, what a fine, strong young woman she was when you knew her. Now when she first came to me she was pale and peaking, afraid of wet feet or an open window; afraid of this, that and the other, always tired, and with no appetite except for sweets. Mutton and exercise made her what you remember; and before she went home to France to marry an old admirer, she thanked me with tears in her eyes for having made her love mutton. She said "love" when she should have said "like"; but I was too proud and pleased to correct her English then; I only answered, "Ah, dear Mademoiselle, always love your husband and love your mutton."'

Lucy had a sweet, plaintive voice, to which her own sweet sorrow now added a certain simple pathos; and when in the twilight she sang 'Alice Grey', or 'She wore a wreath of roses', or some other old favourite, good Miss Drum would sit and listen till the tears gathered behind her spectacles. Were tears in the singer's eyes also? She thought now with more tenderness than ever before of the suitors she had rejected in her hopeful, happy youth, especially of a certain Mr Tresham, who had wished her all happiness as he turned to leave her in his dignified regret. She had always had a great liking for Mr Tresham, and now she could feel for him.

8

On the 28th of June, four letters came to Lucy by the first delivery:

I

My dear Lucy,

Pray do not think me thoughtless if I once more ask whether you will sanction an extension of our holiday. Mrs Tyke presses us to remain with her through July, and Dr Tyke is not less urgent. When I hinted that their hospitality had already been trespassed upon, the Doctor quoted Hone[4] (as he said: I doubt if it is there) –

> 'In July
> No goodbye;
> In August
> Part we must.'

I then suggested that you may be feeling moped at home, and in want of change; but, of course, the Doctor had still an answer ready: 'Tell Lucy from me, that if she takes you away I shall take it very ill, as the homoeopath said when his learned brother substituted cocoa-nibs for champagne.' And all the time Cousin Lucy was begging us to stay, and Jane was looking at me so earnestly: in short, dear Lucy, if 'no' must be said, pray will you say it; for I have been well-nigh talked over.

And, indeed, we must make allowances for Jane, if she seems a little selfish; for, to let you into a secret, I believe she means to accept Mr Durham if he makes her the offer we all are expecting from him. At first I was much displeased at her giving him any encouragement, for it appeared to me impossible that she could view his attentions with serious approbation: but I have since become convinced that she knows

23

her own mind, and is not trifling with him. How it is possible for her to contemplate union with one so unrefined and ostentatious I cannot conceive, but I have no power to restrain her; and when I endeavoured to exert my influence against him, she told me in the plainest terms that she preferred luxury with Mr Durham to dependence without him. Oh, Lucy, Lucy! Have we ever given her cause to resent her position so bitterly? Were she my own child, I do not think I could love her more or care for her more anxiously: but she has never understood me, never done me justice. I speak of myself only, not of you also, because I shall never marry, and all I have has been held simply in trust for her: with you it is, and ought to be, different.

But you must not suffer for Jane's wilfulness. If you are weary of our absence, I really must leave her under Cousin Lucy's care – for she positively declines to accompany me home at present – and return to everyday duties. I am sick enough of pleasuring, I do assure you, as it is; though, were Mr Durham a different man, I should only rejoice, as you may suppose.

Well, as to news, there is not much worth transmitting. Jane has been to the Opera three times, and to the English play once. Mr Durham sends the boxes, and Dr and Mrs Tyke never tire of the theatre. The last time they went to the Opera they brought home with them to supper Mr Tresham, whom you may recollect our meeting here more than once, and who has lately returned to England from the East. Through some misunderstanding he expected to see you instead of me, and looked out of countenance for a moment: then he asked after you, and begged me to remember him to you when I wrote. He appeared much interested in hearing our home news, and concerned when I mentioned that you have seemed less strong lately. Pray send compliments for him when next you write, in case we should see him again.

Mr Hartley I always liked, and now I like his wife also: she is an engaging little thing, and gets us all to call her Stella. You, I am sure, will be fond of her when you know her. How I wish her father resembled her! She is as simple and as merry as a bird, and witnesses Mr Durham's attentions to Jane with perfect equanimity. As to Mr Hartley, he seems as much amused as if the bulk of his wife's enormous fortune were not at stake; yet anyone must see the other man is in earnest. Stella is reckoned a clever actress, and private theatricals of some sort are impending. I say 'of some sort', because Jane, who is indisputably the beauty of our circle, would prefer tableaux vivants; and I know not which will carry her point.

My love to Miss Drum. Don't think me selfish for proposing to remain longer away from you; but, indeed, I am being drawn in two opposite directions by two dear sisters, of whom I only wish that one had as much good sense and good taste as the other.

Your affectionate sister,
– Catherine Charlmont

* * *

II

My dear Lucy,

I know Catherine is writing, and will make the worst of everything, just as if I was cut out to be an old maid.

Surely at my age one may know one's own mind; and, though I'm not going to say before I am asked whether I like Mr Durham, we are all very well aware, my dear Lucy, that I like money and comforts. It's one thing for Catherine and you, who have enough and to spare, to split hairs as to likes and dislikes; but it's quite another for me who have not a penny of my own, thanks to poor dear papa's blindness. Now do be a dear, and tell sister she is welcome to stay this one month more; for, to confess the truth, if I remain here alone I may find myself at my wit's end for a pound or two one of these days. Dress is so dear, and I had rather never go out again than be seen a dowdy; and if we are to have tableaux, I shall want all sorts of things. I don't hold at all with charades and such nonsense, in which people are supposed to be witty; give me a piece in which one's arms are of some use; but of course, Stella, who has no more arm than a pump-handle, votes for theatricals.

The Hartleys are coming today and, of course, Mr Durham, to take us after luncheon to the Crystal Palace. There is a grand concert *coming off, and a flower-show, which would all be yawny enough but for the toilettes. I dare say I shall see something to set me raving; just as last time I was at the Botanic Gardens, I pointed out the loveliest suit of Brussels lace over white silk; but I might as well ask Catherine for wings to fly with.*

Goodbye, my dear Lucy. Don't be cross this once, and when I have a house of my own, I'll do you a good turn.

Your affectionate sister,
– Jane

P.S. I enclose Mr Durham's photograph, which he fished and fished to make me ask for, so at last I begged it to gratify the poor man. Don't you see all Orpingham Place in his speaking countenance?

* * *

III

My dearest Lucy,

You owe me a kindness to balance my disappointment at missing your visit. So please let Catherine know that she and Jane may give us a month more. Dr Tyke wishes it no less than I do, and Mr Durham perhaps more than either of us; but a word to the wise.

Your affectionate cousin,
– Lucy C. Tyke

P.S. The Doctor won't send regards, because he means to write to you himself.

* * *

IV

Dear Lucy,

If you agree with the snail, you find your house just the size for one; and lest bestial example should possess less force than human, I further remind you of what Realmah the Great[5] affirms – 'I met two blockheads, but the one sage kept himself to himself.' All which sets forth to you the charms of solitude, which, as you are such a proper young lady, is of course the only anybody you can be in love with, and of whose society I am bent on affording you prolonged enjoyment.

This can be effected if your sisters stay here for another month, and indeed you must not say us nay; for on your 'yes' hangs a tale which your 'no' may for ever forbid to wag. Miss Catherine looks glummish, but Jenny is all sparkle and roses, like this same month of June; and never is she more sparkling or rosier than when the master of Orpingham Place hails her with that ever fresh remark, 'Fine day, Miss Jane.' Don't nip the summer crops of Orpingham Place in the bud, or, rather, don't retard them by unseasonable frost; for I can't fancy my friend will be put off with anything less than a distinct 'no'; and when it comes to that, I think Miss Jane, in her trepidation, will say 'yes'. And if you are a good girl, and let the little one play out her play, when she has come into the sugar and spice and all that's nice, you shall come to Notting Hill this very next May, and while the sun shines make your hay.

> Your venerable cousin's husband
> (by which I merely mean),
> Your cousin's venerable husband,
> – Francis Tyke, M.D.

N.B. I append M.D. to remind you of my professional status, and so quell you by the weight of my advice.

* * *

Lucy examined the photograph of Mr Durham with a double curiosity, for he was Mr Hartley's father-in-law as well as Jane's presumptive suitor. She looked, and saw a face not badly featured, but vulgar in expression; a figure not amiss, but ill at ease in its studied attitude and superfine clothes. Assuredly it was not George Durham, but the master of Orpingham Place who possessed attractions for Jane; and Lucy felt, for a sister who could be thus attracted, the sting of a humiliation such as her own baseless hopes had never cost her.

Each of her correspondents was answered with judicious variation in the turn of the sentences. To Jane she wrote drily, returning Mr Durham's portrait wrapped in a ten-pound note; an arrangement which, in her eyes, showed a symbolic appropriateness, lost for the moment on her sister. Catherine she answered far more affectionately, begging her on no account to curtail a visit which might be of importance to Jane's prospects; and on the flap of the envelope, she added compliments to Mr Tresham.

9

Mr Tresham had loved Lucy Charlmont sincerely, and until she refused him had entertained a good hope of success. Even at the moment of refusal she avowed the liking for him which all through their acquaintance had been obvious; and then, and not till then, it dawned upon him that her indifference towards himself had its root in preference for another. But he was far too honourable a man either to betray or to aim at verifying his suspicion; and though he continued to visit at Dr Tyke's, where Alan Hartley was so often to be seen idling away time under the comfortable conviction that he was doing no harm to himself or to anyone else, it was neither at once, nor of set purpose, that Arthur Tresham penetrated Lucy's secret. Alan and himself had been college friends; he understood him thoroughly; his ready good nature, which seemed to make everyone a principal person in his regard; his open hand that liked spending; his want of deep or definite purpose; his unconcern as to possible consequences. Then Lucy – in whom Mr Tresham had been on one point woefully mistaken – she was so composed and so cordial to all her friends; there was about her such womanly sweetness, such unpretentious, dignified reserve towards all: her face would light up so brightly when he, or any other, spoke what interested her – not seldom, certainly, when *he* spoke: even after a sort of clue had come into his hands, it was some time before he felt sure of any difference between her manner to Alan and to others. When the conviction forced itself upon him, he grieved more for her than for himself; he knew his friend too intimately to mistake his pleasure in being amused for any anxiety to make himself beloved; he knew about

Alan much that Lucy did not and could not guess, and from the beginning inferred the end.

In the middle of that London season Catherine and Lucy returned to Brompton-on-Sea; and before August had started the main stream of tourists from England to the continent, Mr Tresham packed up his knapsack and, staff in hand, set off on a solitary expedition, of undetermined length, to the East. He was neither a rich nor a poor man; had been called to the Bar, but without pursuing his profession, and was not tied to any given spot; he went away to recruit his spirits and, having recovered them, stayed on out of sheer enjoyment. Yet, when one morning his eye lighted on the Hartley-Durham marriage in the *Times Supplement*, home feeling stirred within him; and he who, twenty-four hours earlier, knew not whether he might not end his days beside the blue Bosporus, on the evening of that same day had started westward.

He felt curious, he would not own to himself that he felt specially interested, to know how Lucy fared; and he felt curious, in a minor degree, to inspect her successful rival.

With himself Lucy had not yet had a rival; not yet, perhaps she might one day, he repeated to himself, only it had not happened yet. And then the sweet, dignified face rose before him kind and cheerful; cheerful still in his memory, though he guessed that now it must look saddened. He had never yet seen it with a settled expression of sadness, and he knew not how to picture it so.

* * *

Mr Drum – or Mr Gawkins Drum, as he scrupulously called himself, on account of a certain Mr Drum, who lived somewhere and went nowhere, and was held by all outsiders to be in his dotage – Miss Drum's brother, Mr Gawkins Drum, had for several years stood as a gay young bachelor of sixty. Not that, strictly speaking, any man (or, alas! any woman) can settle down at sixty and there remain; but at the last of a long series of avowed birthday parties, Mr Drum had drunk his own health as being sixty that very day; this was now some years ago, and still, in neighbourly parlance, Mr Drum was no more than sixty. At sixty-something-indefinite, Gawkins brought home a bride, who confessed to sixty; and all Brompton-on-Sea indulged in a laugh at their expense, till it oozed out that the kindly old couple had gone through all the hopes and disappointments of a many years' engagement, begun at a reasonable age for such matters, and now terminated only because the bedridden brother, to whom the bride had devoted herself during an ordinary lifetime, had at last ended his days in peace. Mr and Mrs Gawkins Drum forestalled their neighbours' laugh by their own, and soon the laugh against them died out, and everyone accepted their house as amongst the pleasantest resorts in Brompton-on-Sea.

Miss Drum, however, felt less leniently towards her brother and sister-in-law, and deliberately regarded them from a shocked point of view. The wedding took place at Richmond, where the bride resided; and the honeymoon came to an end whilst Lucy entertained her old friend, during that long visit at Notting Hill, which promised to colour all Jane's future.

'My dear,' said Miss Drum to her deferential listener; 'my dear, Sarah' – and Lucy felt that that offending Sarah could only be the bride – 'Sarah shall not suffer for Gawkins' folly and her own. I will not fail to visit her in her new home, and to notice her on all proper occasions, but I cannot save her from being ridiculous. I did not wait till I was sixty to make up my mind against wedlock, though perhaps' – and the old lady bridled – 'I also may have endured the preference of some infatuated man. Lucy, my dear, take an old woman's advice: marry, if you mean to marry, before you are sixty, or else remain like myself; otherwise, you make yourself simply ridiculous.'

And Lucy, smiling, assured her that she would either marry before sixty or not at all; and added, with some earnestness, that she did not think she should ever marry. To which Miss Drum answered with stateliness: 'Very well, do one thing or do the other, only do not become ridiculous.'

Yet the old lady softened that evening, when she found herself, as it were, within the radius of the contemned bride. Despite her sixty years – and in truth she looked less than her age – Mrs Gawkins Drum was a personable little woman, with plump red cheeks, gentle eyes, and hair of which the soft brown was threaded, but not overpowered, by grey. There was no affectation of youthfulness in her gown, which was of slate-coloured silk; nor in her cap, which came well on her head; nor in her manner to her guests, which was cordial; nor in her manner to her husband, which was affectionate, with the undemonstrative affectionateness that might now have been appropriate had they married forty years earlier.

Her kiss of welcome was returned frostily by Miss Drum, warmly by Lucy. Mr Drum at first looked a little sheepish under his sister's severe salutation. Soon all were seated at tea.

'Do you take cream and sugar?' asked the bride, looking at her new sister.

'No sugar, I thank you,' was the formal reply. 'And it will be better, Sarah, that you should call me Elizabeth. Though I am an old woman, your years do not render it unsuitable, and I wish to be sisterly.'

'Thank you, dear Elizabeth,' answered Mrs Gawkins, cheerily; 'I hope, indeed, we shall be sisterly. It would be sad times with me if I found I had brought coldness into my new home.'

But Miss Drum would not thaw yet. 'Yes, I have always maintained, and I maintain still, that there must be faults on both sides if a marriage, if any marriage whatever, introduces dissension into a family circle. And I will do my part, Sarah.'

'Yes, indeed' – but Sarah knew not what more to say.

Mr Drum struck in – 'Lucy, my dear' – she had been a little girl perched on his knee when her father asked him years before to be trustee – 'Lucy, my dear, you're not in full bloom. Look at my old lady, and guess: what's a recipe for roses?'

'For shame, Gawkins!' cried both old ladies; one with a smile, the other with a frown.

Still, as the evening wore on, Miss Drum slowly thawed. Having, as it were once for all, placed her hosts in the position of culprits at the moral bar, having sat in judgement on them, and convicted them in the ears of all men (represented by Lucy), she admitted them to mercy, and dismissed them with a qualified pardon. What most softened her towards the offending couple was their unequivocal profession of rheumatism. When she unbendingly declined to remain seated at the supper-table one minute beyond half-past ten, she alleged rheumatism as her impelling motive; and Gawkins and Sarah immediately proclaimed their own rheumatic experience and sympathies. As Miss Drum observed to Lucy on their way home, 'Old people don't confess to rheumatism if they wish to appear young.'

Thus the feud subsided, though Miss Drum to the end of her life occasionally spoke of her sister-in-law as 'that poor silly thing', and of her brother as of one who should have known better.

Whilst, on her side, Mrs Gawkins Drum remarked to her husband, 'What a very old-looking woman that Miss Charlmont is, if she's not thirty, as you say. I never saw such an old, faded-looking woman of her age.'

10

Parties ran high at Kensington and Notting Hill. Stella stood up for charades, Jane for *tableaux*. Mr Hartley naturally sided with his wife, Miss Charlmont held back from volunteering any opinion, Mrs Tyke voted for the last speaker, Dr Tyke ridiculed each alternative; at last Mr Durham ingeniously threw his weight into both scales, and won for both parties a partial triumph. 'Why not,' asked he – 'why not let Pug speak, and Miss Jane be silent?'

This pacific suggestion once adopted, Dr Tyke proposed that a charade word should be fixed upon, and performed by speech or spectacle, as might suit the rival stars; for instance, 'Love apple'.[6]

But who was to be 'love'?

Everybody agreed in rejecting little boys; and Jane, when directly appealed to, refused to represent the Mother of love and laughter; 'for,' as she truly observed, 'that would not be love, after all.' Mr Durham, looking laboriously gallant, aimed at saying something neat and pointed; he failed, yet Jane beamed a smile upon his failure. Then Dr Tyke proposed a plaster Cupid; this, after some disputing, was adopted, with vague accessories of processional Greek girls, to be definitely worked out afterwards. For 'Apple' Alan suggested Paris and the rival goddesses, volunteering himself as Paris: Jane should be Venus, and Catherine would make a capital Juno. Jane accepted her own part as a matter of course, but doubted about her sister. 'Yes,' put in Miss Charlmont, decisively, 'I will be Juno, or anything else which will help us forward a little.' So that was settled; but who should be Minerva? Stella declined to figure as the patroness of wisdom, and Jane drily observed, that they ought all to be tall, or all to be short, in her idea. At last a handsome, not too handsome, friend, Lady Everett, was thought of to take the part. The last scene Dr Tyke protested he should settle himself with Stella, and not be worried any more about it. So those two went into committee together, and Alan edged in ere long for consultation; finally, Miss Charlmont was appealed to, and the matter was arranged amongst them without being divulged to the rest.

But all was peace and plenty, smiles and wax candles, at Kensington, when at last the evening came for the performance. Mrs Hartley's drawing rooms, being much more spacious than Mrs Tyke's, had been chosen for convenience, and about two hundred guests assembled to hear Stella declaim and see Jane attitudinise, as either faction expressed it. Good-natured Mrs Tyke played the hostess, whilst Mrs Hartley remained occult in the green room. Dr Tyke was manager and prompter. Mr Durham, vice Paris-Hartley, welcomed people in a cordial, fussy manner, apologising for the smallness of London rooms, and regretfully alluding to the vast scale of Orpingham Place, 'where a man can be civil to his friends without treading on their toes or their tails – ha! ha!'

But there is a limit to all things – even fussiness has an end. At last everyone worth waiting for had arrived, been received, been refreshed. Orpingham Place died out of the conversation. People exchanged commonplaces, and took their seats; having taken their seats, they exchanged more commonplaces. 'What's the word?' – 'It's such a bore guessing: I never guess anything' – 'People ought to tell the word beforehand' – 'What a horrible man! Is that Mr Hartley?' – 'No, old Durham; backbone Durham' – 'Why backbone?' – 'Don't know; hear him called so' – 'Isn't there a Beauty somewhere?' – 'Don't know; there's the Beast' – and the hackneyed joke received the tribute of a hackneyed laugh.

The manager's bell rang, the curtain drew up.

The plaster cast of Cupid, with fillet, bow, and quiver, on an upholstery pedestal, stood revealed. Music, commencing behind the scenes, approached; a file of English-Grecian maidens, singing and carrying garlands, passed across the stage towards a pasteboard temple, presumably their desired goal, although they glanced at their audience and seemed very independent of Cupid on his pedestal. There were only six young ladies; but they moved slowly, with a tolerable space interposed between each and each, thus producing a processional effect. They sang, in time and in tune, words by Dr Tyke; music (not in harmony, but in unison, to ensure correct execution) by Arthur Tresham:

> '*Love hath a name of Death:*
> *He gives a breath*
> *And takes away.*
> *Lo we, beneath his sway,*
> *Grow like a flower;*
> *To bloom an hour,*
> *To droop a day,*
> *And fade away.*'

The first Anglo-Greek had been chosen for her straight nose, the last for her elegant foot; the intermediate four, possessing good voices, bore the burden of the singing. They all moved and sang with self-complacent ease, but without much dramatic sentiment, except the plainest of the six, who assumed an air of languishment.

Someone suggested 'cupid-ditty,' but without universal acceptance. Someone else, on no obvious grounds, hazarded 'Bore, Wild Boar' – a remark which stung Dr Tyke, as playwright, into retorting, 'Boreas.'[7]

The second scene was dumb show. Alan Hartley as Paris, looking very handsome in a tunic and sandals, and flanked by the largest-sized, woolly toy lambs, sat, apple in hand, awaiting the rival goddesses. A flourish of trumpets announced the entrance of Miss Charlmont, a stately crowned Juno, robed in amber-coloured cashmere, and leading in a leash a peacock, with train displayed, and ingeniously mounted on noiseless wheels. She swept grandly in, and held out one arm, with a studied gesture, for the apple; which, doubtless, would have been handed to her then and there, had not warning notes on a harp ushered in Lady Everett: a modest, sensible-looking Minerva, robed and stockinged in blue, with a funny Athenian owl perched on her shoulder, and a becoming helmet on her head. Paris hesitated visibly, and seemed debating whether or not to split the apple and the difference together, when a hubbub, as of birds singing, chirping, calling, cleverly imitated by Dr Tyke and Stella on water-whistles, heralded the approach of Venus. In she came, beautiful Jane Charlmont, with a steady, gliding step, her eyes kindling with victory, both her small hands outstretched for the apple so indisputably hers, her lips parted in a triumphant smile. Her long, white robe flowed classically to the floor; two doves, seeming to nestle in her hair, billed and almost cooed; but her face eclipsed all beside it; and when Paris, on one knee, deposited the apple within her slim, white fingers, Juno forgot to look indignant and Minerva scornful.

After this, the final scene fell dead and flat. In vain did Stella whisk about as the most coquettish of market-girls of an undefined epoch and country, balancing a fruit-basket on her head, and crying, 'Grapes, melons, peaches, love apples,' with the most natural inflections. In vain did Arthur Tresham beat down the price of peaches, and Alan Hartley bid for love apples: Jane had attained one of her objects, and eclipsed her little friend for that evening.

The *corps dramatique* was to sit down to supper in costume; a point arranged ostensibly for convenience, secretly it may be for vanity's sake: only Stella laid her fruit-basket aside, and Miss Charlmont released her peacock. Lady Everett continued to wear the helmet, which did not conceal her magnificent black hair (she had been a Miss Moss before marriage, Clara Lyon Moss), and Jane retained her pair of doves.

But during the winding up of the charade, more of moment had occurred off the stage than upon it. Jane, her part over, left the other performers to their own devices, and quietly made her way into a conservatory which opened out of the room devoted for that evening to cloaks and hoods. If she expected to be followed she was not disappointed. A heavy step, and an embarrassed clearance of throat, announced Mr Durham. He bustled up to her, where she sat fanning herself and showing white and brilliant against a background of flowers and leaves, whilst he looked at once sheepish and pompous, awkward and self-satisfied; not a lady's man assuredly.

'Hem – haw – Miss Jane, you surpassed yourself. I shall always think of you now as Venus – I shall, indeed.' Jane smiled benignantly. 'Poor Pug's nose is quite out of joint – it is, indeed. But the chit has got a husband, and can snap her fingers at all of us.' Jane surveyed him with grave interrogation, then cast down her lustrous eyes, and slightly turned her shoulder in his direction. Abashed, he resumed: 'But really, Miss Jane, now wasn't Venus a married lady too? and couldn't we –' Jane interrupted him: 'Pray give me your arm, Mr Durham' – she rose: 'let us go back to the company. I don't know what you are talking about, unless you mean to be rude and very unkind' – the voice broke, the large, clear eyes softened to tears; she drew back as he drew nearer. Then Mr Durham, ill-bred, but neither scheming nor cold-hearted – pompous and fussy, but a not ungenerous man for all that – then Mr Durham spoke: 'Don't draw back from me, Miss Jane, but take my arm for once to lead you back to the company, and take my hand for good. For I love and admire you, Miss Jane; and if you will take an oldish man for your husband, you shall never want for money or for pleasure while my name is good in the City.'

Thus in one evening Jane Charlmont attained both her objects.

Supper was a very gay meal, as brilliant as lights, glass, and plate could make it. People were pleased with the night's entertainment, with themselves, and with each other. Mr Durham, with an obtrusive air of festivity, sat down beside Jane, and begged his neighbours not to inconvenience themselves, as they did not mind squeezing. Jane coloured, but judged it too early to frown. Mr Durham, being somewhat old-fashioned, proposed healths: the fair actresses were toasted, the Anglo-Greeks in a bevy, the distinguished stars one by one. Mr Tresham returned thanks for the processional six; Dr Tyke for Miss Charlmont; Sir James Everett and Mr Hartley for their respective wives.

Then Jane's health was drunk: who would rise to return thanks? Mr Durham rose: 'Hem – haw –' said he: 'haw – hem – ladies and gentlemen, allow me to return thanks for the Venus of the evening – I mean for the Venus altogether, whose health you have done me the honour to drink' – knowing smiles circled round the table – 'done us, I should say: not that I unsay what I said – quite the contrary, and I'm not ashamed to have said it. I will only say one word more in thanking you for the honour you have done her and all of us: the champagne corks pop, and suggest popping; but after popping mum's the word. Ladies and gentlemen, my very good friends, I drink your very good health.'

And the master of Orpingham Place sat down.

11

Lucy received the news of Jane's engagement with genuine vexation, and then grew vexed with herself for feeling vexed. Conscience took alarm, and pronounced that envy and pride had a share in her vexation. Self retorted: it is not envy to see that Jane is mercenary, nor pride to dislike vulgarity. Conscience insisted: it is envy to be annoyed by Jane's getting married before you, and it is pride to brand Mr Durham as vulgar, and then taboo him as beyond the pale. Self pleaded: no one likes growing old and being made to feel it; and who would not deprecate a connection who will put one out of countenance at every turn? But Conscience secured the last word: if you were younger than Jane, you would make more allowances for her; and if Mr Durham were engaged to anyone except your sister, you would think it fair not to condemn him as destitute of every virtue because he is underbred.

Thus did Conscience get the better of Self. And Lucy gulped down dignity and disappointment together when, in reply to Miss Drum's 'My dear, I hope your sisters are well, and enjoying their little gaieties,' she said, cheerfully: 'Now, really, you should give me something for such wonderful news: Jane is engaged to be married.'

There was nothing Miss Drum relished more than a wedding 'between persons suited to each other, and not ridiculous on the score of age and appearance', as she would herself pointedly have defined it. Now Jane was obviously young enough and pretty enough to become a bride; so Miss Drum was delighted, and full of interest and of enquiries, which Lucy found it rather difficult to answer satisfactorily.

'And who is the favoured gentleman, my dear?'

'Mr Durham, of Orpingham Place, in Gloucestershire. Very rich it seems, and a widower. His only daughter,' Lucy hurried on with an imperceptible effort, 'married that Mr Hartley Catherine and I used to meet so often at Notting Hill. She was thought to be a great heiress; but I suppose this will make some difference.'

'Then he is rather old for Jane?'

'He is not yet fifty it seems, though of course that is full old. By what he says, Orpingham Place must be a very fine country-seat; and Jane appears cut out for wealth and pleasure, she has such a power of enjoying herself' – and Lucy paused.

Miss Drum, dropping the point of age, resumed: 'Now what Durham will this be, my dear? I used to know a Sir Marcus Durham – a gay, hunting baronet. He was of a north-country family; but this may be a branch of the same stock. He married an earl's daughter, Lady Mary; and she used to take precedence, let who would be in the room, which was not thought to be in very good taste when the dowager Lady Durham was present. Still an earl's daughter ought to understand good breeding, and that was how she acted; I do not wish to express any opinion. Perhaps Mr Durham may have a chance of the baronetcy, for Sir Marcus left no children, but was succeeded by a bachelor brother; and then Jane will be "my lady" some day.'

'No,' replied Lucy; 'I don't think that likely. Mr Durham is enormously wealthy, by what I hear; but not of a county family. He made his fortune in the City.'

Miss Drum persisted: 'The cadets of even noble families have made money by commerce over and over again. It is no disgrace to make a fortune; and I see no reason why Mr Durham should not be a baronet some day. Many a City man has been as fine a gentleman as any idler at court. Very likely Mr Durham is an elegant man of talent, and well connected; if so, a fortune is no drawback, and the question of age may be left to the lady's decision.'

Lucy said no more: only she foresaw and shrank from that approaching day of undeceiving which should bring Mr Durham to Brompton-on-Sea.

Once set off on the subject of family, there was no stopping Miss Drum, who, having had no provable great-grandfather, was sensitive on the score of pedigree.

'You might not suppose it now, Lucy, but it is well known that our family name of Drum, though less euphonious than that of Durham, is in fact the same. I made the observation once to Sir Marcus, and he laughed with pleasure, and often afterwards addressed me as cousin. Lady Mary did not like the suggestion; but no one's fancies can alter a fact' – and the old lady looked stately, and as if the Drum-Durham theory had been adopted and emblazoned by the College of Heralds; whereas, in truth, no one besides herself, not even the easy-tempered Gawkins, held it.

Meanwhile, all went merrily and smoothly at Notting Hill. As Jane had said, she was old enough to know her own mind, and apparently she knew it. When Mr Durham presented her with a set of fine diamonds, she dropped naturally into calling him George; and when he pressed her to name the day, she answered, with an assumption of girlishness, that he must talk over all those dreadful things with Catherine.

To Miss Charlmont he had already opened his mind on the subject of settlements: Jane should have everything handsome and ample, but Pug must not lose her fortune either. This Catherine, deeming it right and reasonable, undertook to explain to Jane. Jane sulked a little to her sister, but displayed only a smiling aspect to her lover, feeling in her secret heart that her own nest was being particularly well feathered: for not only were Mr Durham's new marriage settlements most liberal, in spite of Stella's prospective twenty thousand pounds on coming of age, and twenty thousand at her father's demise; but Catherine, of her own accord, provided that at her death all her share of their father's property should descend to Jane, for her own separate use, and at her own absolute disposal. The younger sister, indeed, observed with safe generosity: 'Suppose you should marry, too, some day?' But Catherine, grateful for any gleam of unselfishness in her favourite sister, answered warmly and decisively: 'I never meant to marry, and I always meant what fortune I had to be yours at last: only, dear, do not again think hardly of our poor father's oversight.'

Mr Durham was urgent to have the wedding day fixed, and Jane reluctant merely and barely for form's sake. A day in August was named, and the honeymoon pre-devoted to Paris and Switzerland. Then Miss Charlmont pronounced it time to return home; and was resolute that the wedding should take place at Brompton-on-Sea, not at Notting Hill as the hospitable Tykes proposed.

Jane was now nothing loath to quit town – Mr Durham unwilling to lose her, yet willing as recognising the step for an unavoidable preliminary. Nevertheless, he felt hurt at Jane's indifference to the short separation; whilst Jane, in her turn, felt worried at his expecting any show of sentiment from her, though, having once fathomed his feelings, she kept the worry to herself and produced the sentiment. He looked genuinely concerned when they parted at London Bridge Station; but Jane never in her life had experienced a greater relief than now, when the starting train left him behind on the platform. A few more days, and it would be too late to leave him behind: but she consoled herself by reflecting that without him she might despair of ever seeing Paris; Switzerland was secondary in her eyes.

Miss Drum had often set as a copy, 'Manners make the Man', and explained to her deferential pupils how in that particular phrase 'Man' includes 'Woman'. Catherine in later life reflected that 'Morals make the Man' (including 'Woman') conveys a not inferior truth. Jane might have modified the sentence a trifle further, in employing it as an M copy, and have written, 'Money makes the Man'.

1 2

Lucy welcomed her sisters home, after an absence of unprecedented duration, with warm-hearted pleasure, but Jane went far to extinguish the feeling.

In the heyday of her blooming youth and satisfaction, she was not likely to acquire any tender tact lacking at other times; and an elder sister, mentally set down in her catalogue of old maids, was fair game.

'Why, Lucy,' she cried, as they sat together the first evening, herself the only idler of the three, 'you look as old as George, and about as lively: Miss Drum must be catching.'

'Do leave Miss Drum alone,' Lucy answered, speaking hastily from a double annoyance. 'And if ' – she forced a laugh – 'surely if my looks recall George to your mind, they ought to please you.'

But Jane was incorrigible. 'My dear, George is Orpingham Place, and Orpingham Place is George; but your looks suggest some distinction between the two. Only think, he expected me to grow dismal at leaving him behind, and I did positively see his red pocket handkerchief fluttering in the breeze as we screamed out of the station. And he actually flattered himself I should not go out much till the wedding is over; catch me staying at home if I can help it! By the by, did you mean a joke by wrapping his photograph up in the ten-pound note? It struck me afterwards as really neat in its way.'

'Oh, Jane!' put in Catherine, and more she might have added in reproof; but at that instant the door opened, and Mr Ballantyne was announced.

Mr Ballantyne was a solicitor, related to Mrs Gawkins Drum, and taken into partnership by that lady's husband shortly before their marriage. Judging by looks, Mr Ballantyne might have been own nephew to Miss Drum rather than to her sister-in-law, so neutral was he in aspect and manner; if ever anyone liked him at first sight, it was because there was nothing on the surface to stir a contrary feeling; and if anyone volunteered a confidence to him, it was justified by his habitual taciturnity, which suggested a mechanical aptitude at keeping a secret; yet, however appearances were against him, he was a shrewd man of business, and not deficient in determination of character.

He arrived by appointment to show Miss Charlmont the draft of her settlement on her sister, and take, if need be, further instructions. She was one to see with her own eyes rather than merely to hear with her own ears, and therefore retired with the papers to the solitude of her own room, leaving her sisters to entertain the visitor.

Thus left, Mr Ballantyne took a respectful look at Jane, whose good luck in securing the master of Orpingham Place he considered rare indeed. Looking at her he arrived at the conclusion that Mr Durham also had been lucky. Jane just glanced at Mr Ballantyne, mentally appraising him as a nonentity; but in that glance she saw his admiration; admiration always propitiated her, and she deigned to be gracious.

Various maiden ladies in Brompton-on-Sea would have been gracious to Mr Ballantyne from a different motive. Though still a youngish man, he was a widower, already in easy circumstances, and with a prospect of growing rich. His regard for his late wife's memory was most decorous, but not such as to keep him inconsolable; and his only child, Frank, being no more than five years old and healthy, need scarcely be viewed as a domestic drawback; indeed, certain spinsters treated the boy with a somewhat demonstrative affection, but these ladies were obviously not in their teens.

Mr Ballantyne meanwhile, though mildly courteous to all, had not singled out anyone for avowed preference. Possibly he liked Miss Edith Sims, a doctor's daughter, a bold equestrian, a first-rate croquet player; she hoped so sincerely, for she had unbecoming carroty hair and freckles; possibly he liked Lucy Charlmont, but she had never given the chance a thought. Of Miss Charlmont, whom he had seen twice, and both times exclusively on business, he stood in perceptible awe.

Catherine, finding nothing to object to in the draft, returned it to Mr Ballantyne with her full assent. Then tea was brought in, and Mr Ballantyne was asked to stay. His aptitude for carrying cups and plates, recognised and admired in other circles, here remained in abeyance, Miss Charlmont adhering to the old fashion of people sitting round the tea table at tea no less formally than round the dining table at dinner.

A plan for a picnic having been set on foot by the Gawkins Drums, Lucy had been invited, and had accepted before Jane's engagement was announced. So now Mr Ballantyne mentioned the picnic, taking for granted that Lucy would join, and empowered by the projectors to ask her sisters also; Jane brightened at the proposal, being secretly charmed at a prospect of appearing amongst her familiar associates as mistress elect of Orpingham Place; but Catherine demurred –

'Thank you, Mr Ballantyne; I will call myself and thank Mrs Drum, but Mr Durham might object, and I will stay at home with my sister. No doubt we shall find future opportunities of all meeting.'

'Dear me!' cried Jane; 'Mr Durham isn't Bluebeard; or, if he is, I had better get a little fun first. My compliments, please, and I shall be too glad to come.'

'Oh, Jane!' remonstrated Miss Charlmont; but it was a hopeless remonstrance. Jane, once bent on amusement, was not to be deterred by doubtful questions of propriety; and the elder sister, mortified, but more anxious for the offender's credit than for her own dignity, changed her mind perforce and, with a sigh, accepted the invitation.

If Jane was determined to go, she had better go under a middle-aged sister's eye; but the party promised to be a large one, including various strange gentlemen, and Catherine honestly judged it objectionable.

Jane, however, was overflowing with glee, and questioned Mr Ballantyne energetically as to who were coming. When he was gone, she held forth to her sisters – 'That hideous Edith Sims, of course she will ride over on Brunette, to show her figure and her bridle hand. I shall wear pink, and sit next her to bring out her freckles. I've not forgotten her telling people I had no fortune. Don't you see she's trying to hook Mr Ballantyne? You heard him say she has been consulting him about something or other. Let's drive Mr Ballantyne over in our carriage, and the baby can perch on the box.'

Lucy said, 'Nonsense, Jane; Mr Ballantyne has his own dog cart, and he is tiresome enough without keeping him all to ourselves.'

And Catherine added, this time peremptorily, 'My dear, that is not to be thought of; I could not justify it to Mr Durham. Either you will drive over with Lucy and me, and any other person I may select, or you must find a carriage for yourself, as I shall not go to the picnic.'

13

The environs of Brompton-on-Sea were rich in spots adapted to picnics, and the Gawkins Drums had chosen the very prettiest of these eligible spots. Rocky Drumble, a green glen of the floweriest, but with fragments of rock showing here and there, possessed an echo point and a dripping well: it was, moreover, accredited by popular tradition with a love-legend and, on the same authority, with a ghost for moonlight nights. Rocky Drumble was threaded from end to end by a stream which nourished watercresses; at one season its banks produced wild strawberries, at another nuts, sometimes mushrooms. All the year round the glen was frequented by songbirds; not seldom a squirrel would scamper up a tree, or a rabbit sit upright on the turf, winking his nose. Rocky Drumble on a sunny summer day was a bower of cool shade, and of a silence heightened, not broken, by sounds of birds and of water, the stream at hand, the sea not far off; a bower of sun-chequered shade, breaths of wind every moment shifting the shadows, and the sun making its way in, now here, now there, with an endless, monotonous changeableness.

On such a day the Charlmonts drove to their rendezvous in Rocky Drumble. The carriage held four inside: Miss Drum and Catherine sitting forward, with Lucy and Jane opposite. On the box beside the driver perched little Frank Ballantyne, very chatty and merry at first; but to be taken inside and let fall asleep when, as was foreseen, he should grow tired. The child had set his heart on going to the picnic, and good Miss Drum had promised to take care of him – Miss Drum nominally, Lucy by secret understanding, for the relief of her old friend.

Miss Drum wore a drawn silk bonnet, which had much in common with the awning of a bathing machine. Catherine surmounted her inevitable cap by a broad-brimmed brown straw hat. Lucy wore a similar hat without any cap under it, but looked, in fact, the elder of the two. Jane, who never sacrificed complexion to fashion, also appeared in a shady hat, dove-coloured, trimmed with green leaves, under which she produced a sort of apple-blossom effect, in a cloud of pink muslin over white, and white *appliquée* again over the pink. Catherine had wished her to dress soberly, but Jane had no notion of obscuring her beauties. She had bargained with Mr Durham that he was not to come down to Brompton-on-Sea till the afternoon before the wedding; and when he looked hurt at her urgency, had assumed an air at once affectionate and reserved, assuring him that this course seemed to her due to the delicacy of their mutual relations. Five days were still wanting to the wedding day, George was not yet inalienably at her elbow, and no moment could appear more favourable for enjoyment. Surely if a skeleton promised to preside at the next banquet, this present feast was all the more to be relished: for though, according to Jane's definition, George was Orpingham Place, she would certainly have entered upon Orpingham Place with added zest had it not entailed George.

Miss Charlmont had delayed starting till the very last moment, not wishing to make more of the picnic than could be helped; and when she with her party reached the Drumble, they found their friends already on the spot. The last-comers were welcomed with a good deal of friendly bustle, and half-a-dozen gentlemen, in scarcely more than as many minutes, were presented to Jane by genial little Mrs Drum, who had never seen her before, and was charmed at first sight. Jane, happily for Catherine's peace of mind, assumed an air of dignity in unison with her distinguished prospects: she was gracious rather than coquettish – gracious to all, but flattering to none; a change from former days, when her manner used to savour of coaxing. Edith Sims had ridden over on Brunette, and Jane, keeping her word as to sitting next her, produced the desired effect.

The Charlmonts coming late, everyone was ready for luncheon on their arrival, and no strolling was permitted before the meal. As to the luncheon, it included everything usual and nothing unusual, and most of the company consuming it displayed fine, healthy appetites. Great attention was paid to Jane, who was beyond all comparison the best-looking woman present; whilst two or three individuals made mistakes between Catherine and Lucy, as to which was Miss Charlmont.

Poor Lucy! She seldom felt more heavy-hearted than now, as she sat talking and laughing. She felt herself getting more and more worn-looking as she talked and laughed on, getting visibly older and more faded. How she wished that Frank, who had fallen asleep on a plaid after stuffing unknown sweets into his system – how she wished that Frank would wake and become troublesome, to give her some occupation less intolerable than 'grinning and bearing'!

Luncheon over, the party broke up, splitting into twos and threes, and scattering themselves here and there through the Drumble. Miss Charlmont attaching herself doggedly to Jane, found herself clambering up and down banks and stony excrescences in company with a very young Viscount and his tutor: as she clambered, exasperation waxed within her at the futility of the young men's conversation and the complacency of Jane's rejoinders; certainly, had anyone been studying Catherine's face (which nobody was), he would have beheld an un-wonted aspect at a picnic.

Miss Drum, ostentatiously aged because in company with her brother and his bride, had chosen before luncheon was well over to wrap herself up very warmly, and ensconce herself for an avowed nap inside one of the flys. 'You can call me for tea,' she observed to Lucy; 'and when Frank tires you, you can leave him in the carriage with me.' But Frank was Lucy's one resource: minding him served as an excuse for not joining Mr Drum, who joked, or Mr Ballantyne, who covertly stared at her, or Edith Sims, who lingering near Mr Ballantyne talked of horses, or any other person whose conversation was more tedious than silence.

When Frank woke, he recollected that nurse had told him straw-berries grew in the Drumble; a fact grasped by him without the drawback of any particular season. Off he started in quest of strawberries, and Lucy zealously started in his wake, not deeming it necessary to undeceive him. The little fellow wandered and peered about diligently awhile after imaginary strawberries; failing these, he suddenly clamoured for a game at hide-and-seek: he would hide, and Lucy must not look.

They were now among the main fragments of rock found in the Drumble, out of sight of their companions. Lucy had scarcely shut her eyes as desired, when a shout of delight made her open them still more quickly, in time to see Frank scampering, as fast as his short legs would carry him, after a scampering rabbit. He was running – she recollected it in an instant – headlong towards the stream, and was already some yards from her. She called after him, but he did not turn, only cried out some unintelligible answer in his babyish treble. Fear lent her speed; she bounded after him, clearing huge stones and brushwood with instinctive accuracy. She caught at his frock – missed it – caught at it again – barely grasped it – and fell, throwing him also down in her fall. She fell on stones and brambles, bruising and scratching herself severely: but the child was safe, and she knew it, before she fainted away, whilst even in fainting her hand remained tightly clenched on his frock.

Frank's frightened cries soon brought friends to their assistance. Lucy, still insensible, was lifted onto smooth turf, and then sprinkled with water till she came to herself. In few words – for she felt giddy and hysterical but was resolute not to give way – she accounted for the accident, blaming herself for having carelessly let the child run into danger. It was impossible for any carriage to drive so far along the

Drumble, so she had to take someone's arm to steady her in walking to meet the fly. Mr Ballantyne, as pale as a sheet, offered his arm; but she preferred Mr Drum's, and leant heavily on it for support.

Lucy was soon safe in the fly by Miss Drum's side, whose nap was brought to a sudden end, and who, waking scared and fidgety, was disposed to lay blame on everyone impartially – beginning with herself, and ending, in a tempered form, with Lucy. The sufferer thus disposed of, and packed for transmission home, the remaining picnickers, influenced by Mrs Drum's obvious bias, declined to linger for rustic tea or other pleasures, and elected then and there to return to their several destinations. The party mustered round the carriages ready to take their seats: but where were Catherine and Jane, Viscount and tutor? Shouting was tried, whistling was tried, 'Cooee' was tried by amateur Australians for the nonce: all in vain. At last Dr Sims stepped into the fly with Lucy, promising to see her safe home; Miss Drum, smelling bottle in hand, sat sternly beside her; Frank, after undergoing a paternal box on the ear, was degraded from the coachman's box to the back seat, opposite the old lady, who turned towards him the aspect as of an ogress: and thus the first carriage started, with Edith reining in Brunette beside it. The others followed without much delay, one carriage being left for the truants; and its driver charged to explain, if possible without alarming the sisters, what had happened to cut short the picnic.

14

The day before the wedding, Lucy announced that she still felt too much bruised and shaken to make one of the party, either at church or at breakfast. Neither sister contradicted her – Catherine, because she thought the excuse valid; Jane, because Lucy, not having yet lost the traces of her accident, must have made but a sorry bridesmaid: and, as Jane truly observed, there were enough without her, for her defection still left a bevy of eight bridesmaids in capital working order.

Brompton-on-Sea possessed only one hotel of any pretensions – 'The Duke's Head', so designated in memory of that solitary Royal Duke who had once made brief sojourn beneath its roof. He found it a simple inn, bearing the name and sign of 'The Three Mermaids' – the mermaids appearing in paint as young persons, with yellow hair and combs, and faces of a type which failed to account for their uninterrupted self-ogling in hand-mirrors; tails were shadowily indicated beneath waves of deepest blue. After the august visit this signboard was superseded by one representing the Duke as a gentleman of inane aspect, pointing towards nothing discoverable; and this work of art, in its turn, gave place to a simple inscription, 'The Duke's Head Hotel'.

Call it by what name you would, it was as snug a house of entertainment as rational man or reasonable beast need desire, with odd little rooms opening out of larger rooms and off staircases; the only trace now visible of the Royal Duke's sojourn (beyond the bare inscription of his title) being royal sentries in coloured pasteboard effigy, the size of life, posted on certain landings and at certain entrances. All the window sills bore green boxes of flowering plants, whence a sweet smell, mostly of mignonette, made its way within doors. The best apartments looked into a square courtyard, turfed along three sides, and frequented by pigeons; and the pigeon-house, standing in a turfy corner, was topped by a bright silvered ball.

The landlord of the 'Duke's Head', a thin, tallowy-complexioned man, with a manner which might also be described as unpleasantly oily or tallowy, was in a bustle that same day, and all his household was bustling around him: for not merely had the 'Duke's Head' undertaken to furnish the Durham-Charlmont wedding breakfast with richness and elegance, but the bridegroom elect, whom report endowed with a pocketful of plums,[8] the great Mr Durham himself, with sundry fashionable friends, was coming down to Brompton-on-Sea by the five-thirty train, and would put up for one night at the 'Duke's Head'. The waiters donned their whitest neckcloths, the waitresses their pinkest caps; the landlady, in crimson gown and gold chain, loomed like a local Mayor; the landlord shone, as it were, snuffed and trimmed: never, since the era of that actual Royal Duke, had the 'Duke's Head' smiled such a welcome.

Mr Durham, stepping out of the carriage onto the railway platform, and followed by Alan Hartley, Stella, and Arthur Tresham, indulged hopes that Jane might be there to meet him, and was disappointed. Not that the matter had undergone no discussion. Miss Charlmont – that unavoidable drive home from the picnic with a young Viscount and a tutor for *vis-à-vis* still rankling in her mind – had said, 'My dear, there would be no impropriety in our meeting George at the station, and he would certainly be gratified.' But Jane had answered, 'Dear me, sister! George will keep, and I've not a moment to spare; only don't stay at home for me.'

So no one met Mr Durham. But when he presented himself at the private house on the esplanade, Jane showed herself all smiling welcome, and made him quite happy by her pretty ways. True, she insisted on his not spending the evening with her; but she hinted so tenderly at such restrictions vanishing on the morrow, and so modestly at remarks people might make if he did stay, that he was compelled to yield the point and depart in great admiration of her reserve, though he could not help recollecting that his first wooing had progressed and prospered without any such amazing proprieties. But then the mother of Everilda Stella had seen the light in a second-floor back room at Gateshead, and had married out of a circle where polite forms were not in the ascendant; whereas Jane Charlmont looked like a duchess, or an angel, or Queen Venus herself, and was altogether a different person. So Mr Durham, discomfited, but acquiescent, retreated to the 'Duke's Head', and there consoled himself with more turtle soup and crusty old port than Dr Tyke would have sanctioned. Unfortunately Dr and Mrs Tyke were not coming down till the latest train that night from London, so Mr Durham gorged unrebuked. He had seen Lucy, and taken rather a fancy to her, in spite of her blemished face, and had pressed her to visit Orpingham Place as soon as ever he and Jane should have returned from the Continent. He preferred Lucy to Catherine, with whom he never felt quite at ease; she was so decided and self-possessed, and so much better bred than himself. Not that Backbone Durham admitted this last point of superiority; he did not acknowledge, but he winced under it. Lucy on her side had found him better than his photograph – and that was something.

After tea she was lying alone on the drawing-room sofa in the pleasant summer twilight; alone, because her sisters were busy over

Jane's matters upstairs; alone with her own thoughts. She was thinking of very old days, and of days not so old and much more full of interest. She tried to think of Jane and her prospects; but against her will Alan Hartley's image intruded itself on her reverie, and she could not banish it. She knew from Mr Durham that he had come down for the wedding; she foresaw that they must meet, and shrank from the ordeal, even whilst she wondered how he would behave and how she herself should behave. Alone, and in the half-darkness, she burned with shamefaced dread of her own possible weakness, and mortified self-love wrung tears from her eyes as she inwardly prayed for help.

The door opened, the maid announced Mr and Mrs Hartley.

Lucy, startled, would have risen to receive them, but Stella was too quick for her and, seizing both her hands, pressed her gently backwards on the sofa. 'Dear Miss Charlmont, you must not make a stranger of me, and my husband is an old friend. Mayn't I call you Lucy?'

So this was Alan's wife, this little, winning woman, still almost a child – this winning woman, who had won the only man Lucy ever cared for. It cost Lucy an effort to answer, and to make her welcome by her name of Stella.

Then Alan came forward and shook hands, looking cordial and handsome, with that kind tone of voice and tenderness of manner which had deceived poor Lucy once, but must never deceive her again. He began talking of their pleasant acquaintanceship in days of yore, of amusements they had shared, of things done together, and things spoken and not forgotten; it required the proof positive of Stella seated there smiling in her hat and scarlet feather, and with the wedding ring on her small hand, to show even now that Alan only meant friendliness, when he might seem to mean so much more.

Lucy revolted under the fascination of his manner; feeling angry with herself that he still could wield power over her fancy, and angry a little with him for having made himself so much to her and no more. She insisted on leaving the sofa, rang the bell for a second edition of tea, and sent up the visitors' names to her sisters. When they came down, she turned as much shoulder as good breeding tolerated towards Alan, and devoted all the attention she could command to Stella. Soon the two were laughing together over some feminine little bit of fun; then Lucy brought out an intricate piece of tatting which, when completed, was to find its way to Notting Hill – the antimacassar of Mr Durham's first visit there being, in fact, her handiwork; and, lastly, Lucy, once more for the moment with pretty pink cheeks and brightened eyes, convoyed her new friend upstairs to inspect Jane's bridal dress, white satin, under Honiton lace.

When the visit was over, and Lucy safe in the privacy of her own room, a sigh of relief escaped her, followed by a sentiment of deep thankfulness; she had met Alan again, and he had disappointed her. Yes, the spectre which had haunted her for weeks past had, at length, been brought face to face and had vanished. Perhaps surprise at his marriage had magnified her apparent disappointment, perhaps dread of continuing to love another woman's husband had imparted a morbid and unreal sensitiveness to her feelings; be this as it might, she had now seen Alan again, and had felt irritated by the very manner that used to charm. In the revulsion of her feelings she was almost ready to deem herself fortunate and Stella pitiable.

She felt excited, exalted, triumphant rather than happy; a little pained and, withal, very glad. Life seemed to glow within her, her blood to course faster and fuller, her heart to throb, lightened of a load. Recollections which she had not dared face alone, Mr Hartley, by recalling, had stripped of their dangerous charm; had stripped of the tenderness she had dreaded, and the sting under which she had writhed; for he was the same, yet not the same. Now, for the first time, she suspected him not indeed of hollowness, but of shallowness.

She threw open her window to the glorious August moon and stars, and, leaning out, drank deep of the cool night air. She ceased to think of persons, of events, of feelings; her whole heart swelled, and became uplifted with a thankfulness altogether new to her, profound, transporting. When at length she slept, it was with moist eyes and smiling lips.

15

The wedding was over. Jane might have looked still prettier but for an unmistakable expression of gratified vanity; Mr Durham might have borne himself still more pompously but for a deep-seated, wordless conviction that his bride and her family looked down upon him. Months of scheming and weeks of fuss had ended in a marriage, to which the one party brought neither refinement nor tact, and the other neither respect nor affection.

Wedding guests, however, do not assemble to witness exhibitions of respect or affection, and may well dispense with tact and refinement when delicacies not in season are provided; therefore, the party on the esplanade waxed gay as befitted the occasion, and expressed itself in toasts of highly improbable import.

The going off was, perhaps, the least successful point of the show. Catherine viewed flinging shoes as superstitious, Jane as vulgar; therefore no shoes were to be flung. Mr Durham might have made head against 'superstitious', but dared not brave 'vulgar' – so he kept to himself the fact that he should hardly feel thoroughly married without a tributary shoe, and meanly echoed Jane's scorn. But Stella, who knew her father's genuine sentiment, chose to ignore 'superstition' and 'vulgarity' alike; so, at the last moment, she snatched off her own slipper, and dexterously hurled it over the carriage, to Jane's disgust (no love was lost between the two young ladies) and to Mr Durham's inward satisfaction.

Lucy had not joined the wedding party, not caring overmuch to see Jane marry the man who served her as a butt; but she peeped wistfully at the going off, with forebodings in her heart – which turned naturally into prayers – for the ill-matched couple. In the evening, however, when many of the party had returned to London, the few real friends and familiar acquaintances who reassembled as Miss Charlmont's guests found Lucy in the drawing room, wrapped up in something gauzily becoming to indicate that she had been ill, and looking thin under her wraps.

In Miss Charlmont's idea a wedding party should be at once mirthful and grave, neither dull nor frivolous. Dancing and cards were frivolous, conversation might prove dull; games were all frivolous except chess, which, being exclusive, favoured general dullness. These points she had impressed several times on Lucy, who was suspected of an inopportune hankering after bagatelle; and who now sat in the snuggest corner of the sofa, feeling shy, and at a loss what topic to start that should appear neither dull nor frivolous.

Dr Tyke relieved her by turning her embarrassment into a fresh channel: what had she been doing to make herself 'look like a turnip-ghost before its candle is lighted?'

'My dear Lucy!' cried Mrs Tyke, loud enough for everybody to hear her, 'you really do look dreadful, as if you were moped to death. You had much better come with the Doctor and me to the Lakes. Now I beg you to say yes, and come.'

Alan heard with good-natured concern; Arthur Tresham heard as if he heard not. But the first greeting had been very cordial between him and Lucy, and he had not seemed to remark her faded face.

'Yes,' resumed Dr Tyke. 'Now that's settled. You pack up tonight and start with us tomorrow, and you shall be doctored with the cream of drugs for nothing.'

But Lucy said the plan was preposterous, and she felt old and lazy.

Mrs Tyke caught her up: 'Old? my dear child! and I feeling young to this day!'

And the Doctor added: 'Why not be preposterous and happy? "*Quel che piace giova*",[9] as our sunny neighbours say. Besides, your excuses are incredible: "Not at home", as the snail answered to the wood-pecker's rap.'

Lucy laughed, but stood firm; Catherine protesting that she should please herself. At last a compromise was struck: Lucy, on her cousins' return from their tour, should go to Notting Hill, and winter there if the change did her good. 'If not,' said she, wearily, 'I shall come home again, to be nursed by Catherine.'

'If not,' said Dr Tyke, gravely for once, 'we may think about our all seeing Naples together.'

Edith Sims, her hair and complexion toned down by candlelight, sat wishing Mr Ballantyne would come and talk to her; and Mr Ballantyne, unmindful of Edith at the other end of the room, sat making up his mind. Before the accident in the Drumble he had thought of Lucy with a certain distinction, since that accident he had felt uncomfortably in her debt, and now he sat reflecting that, once gone for the winter, she might be gone for good so far as himself was concerned. She was nice-looking and amiable; she was tender towards little motherless Frank; her fortune stood above rather than below what he had proposed to himself in a second wife: if Edith could have read his thoughts, she would have smiled less complacently when at last he crossed over to talk to her of Brunette and investments, and when later still he handed her in to supper. As it was, candlelight and content became her, and she looked her best.

Mrs Gawkins Drum, beaming with good will, and harmonious in silver-grey moire under old point lace, contrasted favourably with her angular sister-in-law, whose strict truthfulness forbade her looking congratulatory: for now that she had seen the 'elegant man of talent' of her previsions, she could not but think that Jane had married his moneybags rather than himself: therefore Miss Drum looked severe and, when viewed in the light of a wedding guest, ominous.

Catherine, no less conscientious than her old friend, took an opposite line, and laboured her very utmost to hide mortification and misgivings, and to show forth that cheerful hospitality which befitted the occasion when contemplated from an ideal point of view; but ease was not amongst her natural gifts, and she failed to acquire it on the spur of an uneasy moment. 'Manners make the Man', 'Morals make the Man', kept running obstinately in her head, and she could not fit Mr Durham to either sentence. In all Brompton-on Sea there was no heavier heart that night than Catherine Charlmont's.

16

November had come, the Tykes were settled at home again, and Lucy Charlmont sat in a railway carriage on her way from Brompton-on-Sea to Notting Hill. Wrapped up in furs, and with a novel open on her lap, she looked very snug in her corner; she looked, moreover, plumper and brighter than at Jane's wedding party. But her expression of unmistakable amusement was not derived from the novel lying unread in her lap: it had its source in recollections of Mr Ballantyne, who had made her an offer the day before, and who had obviously been taken aback when she rejected his suit. All her proneness to bring herself in in the wrong could not make her fear that she had even for one moment said or done, looked or thought, what ought to have misled him: therefore conscience felt at ease, and the comic side of his demeanour remained to amuse her, despite a decorous wish to feel sorry for him. He had looked so particularly unimpulsive in the act of proposing, and then had appeared so much more disconcerted than grieved at her positive 'No', and had hinted so broadly that he hoped she would not talk about his offer, that she could not imagine the matter very serious to him: and if not to him, assuredly to nobody else. 'I dare say it will be Edith Sims at last,' mused she, and wished them both well.

A year earlier, his offer might have been a matter of mere indifference to her, but not now; for her birthday was just over, and it was gratifying to find herself not obsolete even at thirty. This birthday had loomed before her threateningly for months past, but now it was over; and it became a sensible relief to feel and look at thirty very much as she had felt and looked at twenty-nine. Her mirror bore witness to no glaring accession of age having come upon her in a single night. 'After all,' she mused, 'life isn't over at thirty.' Her thoughts flew before her to Notting Hill; if they dwelt on anyone in especial, it was not on Alan Hartley.

Not on Alan Hartley, though she foresaw that they must meet frequently; for he and Stella were at Kensington again, planning to stay there over Christmas. Stella she rather liked than disliked; and as she no longer deemed her lot enviable, to see more of her would be no grievance. Mr Tresham also was in London, and likely to remain there; for since his return from the East he had taken himself to task for idleness, and had joined a band of good men in an effort to visit and relieve the East-End poor in their squalid homes. His hobby happened to be emigration, but he did not ride his hobby roughshod over his destitute neighbours. He was in London hard at work, and by no means faring sumptuously every day; but glad sometimes to get a mouthful of pure night air and of something more substantial at Notting Hill. He and Lucy had not merely renewed acquaintance at the wedding party, but had met more than once afterwards during a week's holiday he gave himself at the seaside; had met on the beach, or in country lanes, or down in some of the many drumbles. They had botanised in company; and one day had captured a cuttlefish together, which Lucy insisted on putting safe back into the sea before they turned homewards. They had talked of what grew at their feet or lay before their eyes; but neither of them had alluded to those old days when first they had known and liked each other, though they obviously liked each other still.

Lucy, her thoughts running on someone who was not Alan, would have made a very pretty picture. A sort of latent smile pervaded her features without deranging them, and her eyes, gazing out at the dreary autumn branches, looked absent and soft; soft, tender, and pleased, though with a wistful expression through all.

The short, winter-like day had darkened by the time London Bridge was reached. Lucy stepped onto the platform in hopes of being claimed by Dr Tyke's man; but no such functionary appeared, neither was the fat coachman discernible along the line of vehicles awaiting occupants. It was the first time Lucy had arrived in London without being either accompanied or met at the station, and the novel position made her feel shy and a little nervous; so she was glad to stand unobtrusively against a wall, whilst more enterprising individuals found or missed their luggage. She preferred waiting, and she had to wait whilst passengers craned their necks, elbowed their neighbours, blundered, bawled, worried the company's servants, and found everything correct after all. At last the huge mass of luggage dwindled to three boxes, one carpet bag, and one hamper, which were Lucy's own; and which, with herself, a porter consigned to a cab. Thus ended her anxieties.

From London Bridge to Notting Hill the cabman of course knew his way, but in the mazes of Notting Hill he appealed to his fare for guidance. Lucy informed him that Apple Trees House stood in its own large garden, and was sure to be well lighted up; and that it lay somewhere to the left, up a steepish hill. A few wrong turnings first made and next retrieved, a few lucky guesses, brought them to a garden wall, which a passing postman told them belonged to Dr Tyke's premises. Lucy thrust her head out, and thought it all looked very like, except that the house itself stood enveloped in grim darkness; she had never noticed it look so dark before: could it be that she had been forgotten and everyone had gone out?

They drove round the little sweep and knocked; waited, and knocked again. It was not till the grumbling cabman had knocked loud and long a third time that the door was opened by a crying maidservant, who admitted Lucy into the unlighted hall with the explanation: 'O Miss, Miss, master has had a fit, and mistress is taking on so you can hear her all over the place.' At the same instant a peal of screaming, hysterical laughter rang through the house.

Without waiting for a candle, Lucy ran stumbling up the broad staircase, guided at once by her familiarity with the house and by her cousin's screams. On the second-floor landing one door stood open revealing light at last, and Lucy ran straight in amongst the lights and the people. For a moment she was dazzled, and distinguished nothing clearly: in another moment she saw and understood all. Arthur Tresham and a strange gentleman were standing pale and silent at the fireplace, an old servant, stooping over the pillows, was busied in some noiseless way, and Mrs Tyke had flung herself face downwards on the bed beside her husband.

Her husband? No, not her husband any longer, for she was a widow.

17

A week of darkened windows, of condolence cards and hushed enquiries, of voices and faces saddened, of footsteps treading softly on one landing. A week of many tears and quiet sorrow; of many words, for in some persons grief speaks; and of half-silent sympathy, for in some even sympathy is silent. A week wherein to weigh this world and find it wanting, wherein also to realise the far more exceeding weight of the other. A week begun with the hope whose blossom goes up as dust, and ending with the sure and certain hope of the resurrection.

In goods and chattels, Mrs Tyke remained none the poorer for her husband's death. He had left almost everything to her and absolutely at her disposal, well knowing that their old faithful servants were no less dear to her than to himself, and having on his side no poor relations to provide for. His nephew Alan Hartley, and Mr Tresham, were appointed his executors. Alan the good-natured, addicted to shirking trouble in general, consistently shirked this official trouble in particular. Arthur Tresham did what little work there was to do, and did it in such a way as veiled his friend's shortcomings. Mrs Tyke, with a lifelong habit of leaning on someone, came, as a matter of course, to lean on him, and appealed to him as to all sorts of details, without once considering whether the time he devoted to her service was reclaimed out of his work, or leisure, or rest; he best knew, and the knowledge remained with him. Alan, though sincerely sorry for his uncle's death, cut private jokes with Stella about his co-executor's frequent visits to Apple Trees House, and ignored the shortcomings which entailed their necessity.

Mrs Tyke, in her bereavement, clung to Lucy, and was thoroughly amiable and helpless. She would sit for hours over the fire, talking and crying her eyes and her nose red, whilst Lucy wrote her letters, or grappled with her bills. Then they would both grow sleepy, and doze off in opposite chimney corners. So the maid might find them when she brought up tea, or so Arthur when he dropped in on business, or possibly on pleasure. Mrs Tyke would sometimes merely open sleepy eyes, shake hands, and doze off again; but Lucy would sit up wide awake in a moment, ready to listen to all his long stories about his poor people. Soon she took to making things for them, which he carried away in his pocket, or, when too bulky for his pocket, in a parcel under his arm. At last it happened that they began talking of old days, before he went to the East, and then each found that the other remembered a great deal about those old days. So gradually it came to pass that, from looking back together, they took also to looking forward together.

Lucy's courtship was most prosaic. Old women's flannel and old men's rheumatism alternated with some more usual details of love-making, and the exchange of rings was avowedly an exchange of old rings. Arthur presented Lucy with his mother's wedding guard; but Lucy gave him a fine diamond solitaire which had been her father's, and the romantic corner of her heart was gratified by the inequality of the gifts. She would have preferred a little more romance certainly on his side; if not less sense, at least more sentiment; something reasonable enough to be relied upon, yet unreasonable enough to be flattering. 'But one cannot have everything,' she reflected, meekly remembering her own thirty years; and she felt what a deep resting place she had found in Arthur's trusty heart, and how shallow a grace had been the flattering charm of Alan's manner. Till, weighing her second love against her first, tears, at once proud and humble, filled her eyes, and 'one cannot have everything' was forgotten in 'I can never give him back half enough'.

After the exchange of rings, she announced her engagement to Catherine and Mrs Tyke; to Jane also and Mr Durham in few words; and as all business connected with Dr Tyke's will was already satis-factorily settled, and Apple Trees House about to pass into fresh hands, she prepared to return home. Mrs Tyke, too purposeless to be aban-doned to her own resources, begged an invitation to Brompton-on-Sea, and received a cordial welcome down from both sisters. Arthur was to remain at work in London till after Easter, and then to join his friends at the seaside, claim his bride, and take her away to spend their honeymoon beside that beautiful blue Bosporus which had not made him forget her.

If there was a romantic moment in their courtship, it was the moment of parting at the noisy, dirty, crowded railway station, when Arthur terrified Lucy, to her great delight, by standing on the carriage-step, and holding her hand locked fast in his own, an instant after the train had started.

18

A short chapter makes fitting close to a short story.

In mid-May, on a morning which set forth the perfection either of sunny spring warmth or of breezy summer freshness, Arthur Tresham and Lucy Charlmont took each other for better, for worse, till death should them part. Mr Gawkins Drum gave away the bride; Miss Drum appeared auspicious as a rainbow; Catherine glowed and expanded with unselfish happiness; Mrs Gawkins Drum pronounced the bride graceful, elegant, but old-looking; Mr Durham contributed a costly wedding present, accompanied by a speech both ostentatious and affectionate; Jane displayed herself a little disdainful, a little cross, and supremely handsome; Alan and Stella – there was a young Alan now, a comical little fright, more like mother than father – Alan and Stella seemed to enjoy their friends' wedding as light-heartedly as they had enjoyed their own. No tears were shed, no stereotyped hypocrisies uttered, no shoes flung; this time a true man and a true woman who loved and honoured each other, and whom no man should put asunder, were joined together; and thus the case did not lend itself to any tribute of lies, miscalled white.

Four months after their marriage, Mr Tresham was hard at work again in London among his East-End poor, while Lucy, taking a day's holiday at Brompton-on-Sea, sat in the old familiar drawing room, Catherine's exclusively now. She had returned from the East blooming, vigorous, full of gentle fun and kindly happiness: so happy that she would not have exchanged her present lot for aught except her own future; so happy that it saddened her to believe Catherine less happy than herself.

The two sisters sat at the open window, alike yet unlike: the elder handsome, resolute, composed; the younger with the old wistful expression in her tender beautiful eyes. They had talked of Jane, who, though not dissatisfied with her lot, too obviously despised her husband; once, lately, she had written of him as the 'habitation tax' paid for Orpingham Place: of Jane, who was too worldly either to keep right in the spirit, or go wrong in the letter. They had talked, and they had fallen silent; for Catherine, who loved no one on earth as she loved her frivolous sister, could best bear in silence the sting of shame and grief for her sake.

Full in view of the drawing-room windows spread the sea, beautiful, strong, resistless, murmuring; the sea which had cast a burden on Catherine's life, and from which she now never meant to absent herself; the sea from which Lucy had fled in the paroxysm of her nervous misery.

At last Lucy spoke again very earnestly – 'Oh, Catherine, I cannot bear to be so happy when I think of you! If only you, too, had a future.'

Catherine leant over her happy sister and gave her one kiss, a rare sign with her of affectionate emotion. Then she turned to face the open sky and sea – 'My dear,' she answered, whilst her eyes gazed beyond clouds and waves, and rested on one narrow streak of sunlight which glowed at the horizon – 'my dear, my future seems further off than yours; but I certainly have a future, and I can wait.'

The Lost Titian

A lie with a circumstance
(Walter Scott)

The last touch was laid on. The great painter stood opposite the masterpiece of the period – the masterpiece of his life.

Nothing remained to be added. The orange drapery was perfect in its fruitlike intensity of hue; each vine leaf was curved, each tendril twisted, as if fanned by the soft south wind; the sunshine brooded drowsily upon every dell and swelling upland: but a tenfold drowsiness slept in the cedar shadows. Look a moment, and those cymbals must clash, that panther bound forward; draw nearer, and the songs of those ripe, winy lips must become audible.

The achievement of his life glowed upon the easel, and Titian was satisfied.

Beside him, witnesses of his triumph, stood his two friends – Gianni the successful, and Giannuccione the universal disappointment.

Gianni ranked second in Venice; second in most things, but in nothing first. His *colorito*[10] paled only before that of his illustrious rival, whose supremacy, however, he ostentatiously asserted. So in other matters. Only the renowned Messer Cecchino was a more sonorous singer; only fire-eating Prince Barbuto a better swordsman; only Arrigo il Biondo a finer dancer or more sculpturesque beauty; even Caterina Suprema, in that contest of gallantry which has been celebrated by so many pens and pencils, though she awarded the rose of honour to Matteo Grande, the wit, yet plucked off a leaf for the all but victor Gianni.

A step behind him lounged Giannuccione, who had promised everything and fulfilled nothing. At the appearance of his first picture – 'Venus whipping Cupid with feathers plucked from his own wing' – Venice rang with his praises, and Titian foreboded a rival: but when, year after year, his works appeared still lazily imperfect, though always all but perfect, Venice subsided in apathetic silence, and Titian felt that no successor to his throne had as yet achieved the purple.

So these two stood with the great master in the hour of his triumph: Gianni loud, and Giannuccione hearty, in his applauses.

Only these two stood with him: as yet Venice at large knew not what her favourite had produced. It was indeed rumoured that Titian had long been at work on a painting which he himself accounted his masterpiece, but its subject was a secret; and while some spoke of it as an undoubted 'Vintage of red grapes', others maintained it to be a 'Dance of wood nymphs'; while one old gossip whispered that, whatever else the painting might contain, she knew whose sunset-coloured tresses and white brow would figure in the foreground. But the general ignorance mattered little; for, though words might have named the theme, no words could have described a picture which combined the softness of a dove's breast with the intensity of an October sunset: a picture of which the light almost warmed, and the fruit actually bloomed and tempted.

Titian gazed upon his work, and was satisfied: Giannuccione gazed upon his friend's work, and was satisfied: only Gianni gazed upon his friend and upon his work, and was enviously dissatisfied.

'Tomorrow,' said Titian – 'tomorrow Venice shall behold what she has long honoured by her curiosity. Tomorrow, with music and festivity, the unknown shall be unveiled; and you, my friends, shall withdraw the curtain.'

The two friends assented.

'Tomorrow,' he continued, half amused, half thoughtful, 'I know whose white brows will be knit, and whose red lips will pout. Well, they shall have their turn: but blue eyes are not always in season; hazel eyes, like hazelnuts, have their season also.'

'True,' chimed the chorus.

'But tonight,' he pursued, 'let us devote the hours to sacred friendship. Let us with songs and bumpers rehearse tomorrow's festivities, and let your congratulations forestall its triumphs.'

'Yes, *evviva*!'[11] returned the chorus, briskly; and again '*evviva*!'

So, with smiles and embraces, they parted. So they met again at the welcome coming of Argus-eyed night.

The studio was elegant with clusters of flowers, sumptuous with crimson, gold-bordered hangings, and luxurious with cushions and perfumes. From the walls peeped pictured fruit and fruitlike faces, between the curtains and in the corners gleamed moonlight-tinted statues; whilst on the easel reposed the beauty of the evening, overhung by budding boughs, and illuminated by an alabaster lamp burning scented oil. Strewn about the apartment lay musical instruments and packs of cards. On the table were silver dishes, filled with leaves and choice fruits; wonderful vessels of Venetian glass, containing rare wines and iced waters; and footless goblets, which allowed the guest no choice but to drain his bumper.

That night the bumpers brimmed. Toast after toast was quaffed to the success of tomorrow, the exaltation of the unveiled beauty, the triumph of its author.

At last Giannuccione, flushed and sparkling, rose: 'Let us drink,' he cried, 'to our host's success tomorrow: may it be greater than the past, and less than the future!'

'Not so,' answered Titian, suddenly; 'not so: I feel my star culminate.'

He said it gravely, pushing back his seat, and rising from table. His spirits seemed in a moment to flag, and he looked pale in the moonlight. It was as though the blight of the evil eye had fallen upon him.

Gianni saw his disquiet, and laboured to remove it. He took a lute from the floor and, tuning it, exerted his skill in music. He wrung from the strings cries of passion, desolate sobs, a wail as of one abandoned, plaintive, most tender tones as of the *solitario passero*.[12] The charm worked: vague uneasiness was melting into delicious melancholy. He redoubled his efforts; he drew out tinkling notes joyful as the feet of dancers; he struck notes like fire and, uniting his voice to the instrument, sang the glories of Venice and of Titian. His voice, full, mellow, exultant, vibrated through the room; and, when it ceased, the bravos of his friends rang out an enthusiastic chorus.

Then, more stirring than the snap of castanets on dexterous fingers; more fascinating, more ominous than a snake's rattle, sounded the music of the dice-box.

The stakes were high, waxing higher and higher; the tide of fortune set steadily towards Titian. Giannuccione laughed and played, played and laughed with reckless good nature, doubling and redoubling his bets apparently quite at random. At length, however, he paused, yawned, laid down the dice, observing that it would cost him a good six months' toil to pay off his losses – a remark which elicited a peculiar smile of intelligence from his companions – and, lounging back upon the cushions, fell fast asleep.

Gianni also had been a loser: Gianni the imperturbable, who won and lost alike with steady hand and unvarying colour. Rumour stated that one evening he lost, won back, lost once more, and finally regained his whole property unmoved: at last only relinquishing the game, which fascinated, but could not excite him, for lack of an adversary.

In like manner he now threw his possessions – as coolly as if they had been another's – piecemeal into the gulf. First his money went, then his collection of choice sketches; his gondola followed, his plate, his jewellery. These gone, for the first time he laughed.

'Come,' he said, '*amico mio*,[13] let us throw the crowning cast. I stake thereon myself; if you win, you may sell me to the Moor tomorrow, with the remnant of my patrimony; to wit, one house, containing various articles of furniture and apparel; yea, if aught else remains to me, that also do I stake: against these set you your newborn beauty, and let us throw for the last time; lest it be said cogged dice[14] are used in Venice, and I be taunted with the true proverb – "Save me from my friends, and I will take care of my enemies."'

'So be it,' mused Titian, 'even so. If I gain, my friend shall not suffer; if I lose, I can but buy back my treasure with this night's winnings. His whole fortune will stand Gianni in more stead than my picture; moreover, luck favours me. Besides, it can only be that my friend jests, and would try my confidence.'

So argued Titian, heated by success, by wine and play. But for these, he would freely have restored his adversary's fortune, though it had been multiplied tenfold, and again tenfold, rather than have risked his life's labour on the hazard of the dice.

They threw.

Luck had turned, and Gianni was successful.

Titian, nothing doubting, laughed as he looked up from the table into his companion's face; but no shadow of jesting lingered there. Their eyes met, and read each other's heart at a glance.

One discerned the gnawing envy of a life satiated: a thousand mortifications, a thousand inferiorities, compensated in a moment.

The other read an indignation that even yet scarcely realised the treachery which kindled it – a noble indignation, that more upbraided the false friend than the destroyer of a life's hope.

It was a nine-days' wonder in Venice what had become of Titian's masterpiece, who had spirited it away, why, when, and where. Some explained the mystery by hinting that Clementina Beneplacida, having gained secret access to the great master's studio, had there, by dint of scissors, avenged her slighted beauty, and in effigy defaced her nut-brown rival. Others said that Giannuccione, paying tipsy homage to his friend's performance, had marred its yet moist surface. Others again averred that in a moment of impatience, Titian's own sponge, flung against the canvas, had irremediably blurred the principal figure. None knew, none guessed the truth. Wonder fulfilled its little day, and then, subsiding, was forgotten: having, it may be after all, as truly amused Venice the volatile as any work of art could have done, though it had robbed sunset of its glow, its glory and its fire.

But why was the infamy of that night kept secret?

By Titian, because in blazoning abroad his companion's treachery, he would subject himself to the pity of those from whom he scarcely accepted homage; and, in branding Gianni as a traitor, he would expose himself as a dupe.

By Gianni, because had the truth got wind, his iniquitous prize might have been wrested from him, and his malice frustrated in the moment of triumph; not to mention that vengeance had a subtler relish when it kept back a successful rival from the pinnacle of fame than when it merely exposed a friend to humiliation. As artists, they might possibly have been accounted rivals; as astute men of the world, never.

Giannuccione had not witnessed all the transactions of that night. Thanks to his drunken sleep, he knew little; and what he guessed, Titian's urgency induced him to suppress. It was indeed noticed how, from that time forward, two of the three inseparables appeared in a measure estranged from the third; yet all outward observances of courtesy were continued and, if embraces had ceased, bows and doffings never failed.

For weeks, even for months, Gianni restrained his love for play and, painting diligently, laboured to rebuild his shattered fortune. All prospered in his hands. His sketches sold with unprecedented readiness, his epigrams charmed the noblest dinner-givers, his verses and piquant little airs won him admission into the most exclusive circles. Withal, he seemed to be steadying. His name no more pointed stories of drunken frolics in the purlieus of the city, of mad wagers in the meanest company, of reckless duels with nameless adversaries. If now he committed follies, they were committed in the best society; if he sinned, it was at any rate in a patrician *casa*;[15] and, though his morals might not yet be flawless, his taste was unimpeachable. His boon companions grumbled, yet could not afford to dispense with him; his warmest friends revived hopes which long ago had died away into despair. It was the heyday of his life: fortune and Venice alike courted him; he had but to sun himself in their smiles, and accept their favours.

So, nothing loath, he did, and for a while prospered. But, as the extraordinary stimulus flagged, the extraordinary energy flagged with it. Leisure returned, and with leisure the allurements of old pursuits. In proportion as his expenditure increased, his gains lessened; and, just when all his property, in fact, belonged to his creditors, he put the finishing stroke to his obvious ruin, by staking and losing at the gambling table what was no longer his own.

That night beheld Gianni grave, dignified, imperturbable, and a beggar. Next day, his creditors, princely and plebeian, would be upon him: everything must go – not a scrap, not a fragment could be held back. Even Titian's masterpiece would be claimed – that prize for which he had played away his soul, by which, it may be, he had hoped to acquire a worldwide fame, when its mighty author should be silenced for ever in the dust.

Yet tomorrow, not tonight, would be the day of reckoning; tonight, therefore, was his own. With a cool head he conceived, with a steady hand he executed, his purpose. Taking coarse pigments, such as, when he pleased, might easily be removed, he daubed over those figures which seemed to live, and that wonderful background, which not Titian himself could reproduce; then, on the blank surface, he painted a dragon, flaming, clawed, preposterous. One day he would recover his dragon, recover his Titian under the dragon, and the world should see.

Next morning the crisis came.

After all, Gianni's effects were worth more than had been supposed. They included Giannuccione's 'Venus whipping Cupid' – how obtained, who knows? – a curiously wrought cup, by a Florentine goldsmith, just then rising into notice; within the hollow of the foot was engraved 'Benvenuto Cellini',[16] surmounted by an outstretched hand, symbolic of welcome, and quaintly allusive to the name; a dab by Giorgione,[17] a scribble of the brush by Titian, and two feet square of genuine Tintoretto.[18] The creditors brightened; there was not enough for honesty, but there was ample for the production of a most decorous bankrupt.

His wardrobe was a study of colour; his trinkets, few but choice, were of priceless good taste. Moreover, his demeanour was unimpeachable and his delinquencies came to light with the best grace imaginable. Some called him a defaulter, but all admitted he was a thorough gentleman.

Foremost in the hostile ranks stood Titian; Titian, who now, for the first time since that fatal evening, crossed his rival's threshold. His eye searched eagerly among the heap of nameless canvases for one unforgotten beauty, who had occasioned him such sore heartache; but he sought in vain; only in the forefront sprawled a dragon – flaming, clawed, preposterous – grinned, twinkled, erected his tail, and flouted him.

'Yes,' said Gianni, answering his looks, not words, yet seeming to address the whole circle, '*Signori miei*,[19] these compose all my gallery. An immortal sketch, by Messer Tiziano'[20] – here a complimentary bow – 'a veritable Giorgione; your own work, Messer Robusti,[21] which needs no comment of mine to fix its value. A few productions by feebler hands, yet not devoid of merit. These are all. The most precious part of my collection was destroyed (I need not state, accidentally) three days ago by fire. That dragon, yet moist, was designed for mine host, Bevilacqua Mangiaruva; but this morning I hear, with deep concern, of his sudden demise.'

Here Lupo Vorace[22] of the *Orco decapitato* stepped forward. He, as he explained at length, was a man of few words (this, doubtless, in theory); but to make a long story short, so charmed was he by the scaly monster that he would change his sign, accept the ownerless dragon, and thereby wipe out a voluminous score which stood against his debtor. Gianni, with courteous thanks, explained that the dragon, still moist, was unfit for immediate transport; that it should remain in the studio for a short time longer; and that, as soon as its safety permitted, he would himself convey it to the inn of his liberal creditor. But on this point Lupo was inflexible. In diffuse but unvarying terms he claimed instant possession of Gianni's master stroke. He seized it, reared it face upwards onto his head, and by his exit broke up the conclave of creditors.

What remains can be briefly told.

Titian, his last hope in this direction wrecked, returned to achieve, indeed, fresh greatnesses: but not the less returned to the tedium of straining after an ideal once achieved, but now lost for ever. Giannuccione, half amused, half mortified at the slighting mention made of his performances, revenged himself in an epigram, of which the following is a free translation:

> *Gianni my friend and I both strove to excel,*
> *But, missing better, settled down in well.*
> *Both fail, indeed; but not alike we fail –*
> *My forte being Venus' face, and his a dragon's tail.*

Gianni, in his ruin, took refuge with a former friend; and there, treated almost on the footing of a friend, employed his superabundant leisure in concocting a dragon superior in all points to its predecessor; but, when this was almost completed, this which was to ransom his unsuspected treasure from the clutches of Lupo, the more relentless clutches of death fastened upon himself.

His secret died with him.

An oral tradition of a somewhere extant lost Titian having survived all historical accuracy, and so descended to another age, misled the learned Dr Landay into purchasing a spurious work for the Gallery of Lunenburg; and even more recently induced Dr Dreieck to expend a large sum on a nominal Titian, which he afterwards bequeathed to the National Museum of Saxe Eulenstein. The subject of this latter painting is a 'Vintage of red grapes', full of life and vigour, exhibiting marked talent, but clearly assignable to the commencement of a later century.

There remains, however, a hope that some happy accident may yet restore to the world the masterpiece of one of her most brilliant sons.

Reader, should you chance to discern over wayside inn or metropolitan hotel a dragon pendent, or should you find such an effigy amid the lumber of a broker's shop – whether it be red, green, or piebald – demand it importunately, pay for it liberally, and in the privacy of home scrub it. It *may* be that from behind the dragon will emerge a fair one, fairer than Andromeda,[23] and that to you will appertain the honour of yet further exalting Titian's greatness in the eyes of a world.

Vanna's Twins

There I stood on the platform at H***, girt by my three boxes, one carpet bag, strapful of shawls and bundle of umbrellas; there I stood, with a courteous stationmaster and two civil porters assuring me that not one lodging was vacant throughout H***. At another time such an announcement might not have greatly signified, for London, whence I came, was less than three hours off; but on this particular occasion it did matter because I was weakened by recent illness, the journey down had shaken me, I was hungry and thirsty for my tea and, through fear of catching cold, I had wrapped up overmuch; so that when those polite officials stated that they could not point out a lodging for me, I felt more inclined to cry than I hope anybody suspected. One of the porters, noticing how pale and weak I looked, good-naturedly volunteered to go to the three best hotels, and see whether in one of them I could be housed for the moment; and though the expensiveness of such a plan secretly dismayed me, I saw nothing better than to accept his offer. Meanwhile, I retreated into the waiting room wishing him success, but wondering, should he not succeed, what would become of me for the night.

Happily for me, my troubles were not aggravated by imaginary difficulties. I was turned forty-five, and looked not a day younger; an age at which there is nothing alarming in finding oneself alone in a strange place, or compelled to take a night journey by rail. So I sat on the waiting-room sofa, shut my eyes to ease, if possible, a racking headache, and made up my mind that, at the worst, I could always take the mail-train back to London.

After all, I had not long to wait. Within ten minutes of leaving me, my porter returned with the news that, if I did not mind a very unfashionable, but quite respectable, quarter of H***, he had just heard of a first floor vacated half an hour before my arrival, and ready, if I pleased, to receive me. I merely asked, was it clean? and being assured that there was not a tidier young woman in all H*** than 'Fanny', that her husband was a decent optician and stonecutter, and that for cleanliness any of their floors might be eaten off, I felt only too thankful to step into a fly and accompany my boxes to an abiding place. Before starting, I happened to ask the name of my landlord, and was answered somewhat vaguely by my porter, 'We call them Cole.'

The report of a coming lodger had travelled before me, and I found Mr Cole and his Fanny awaiting me at their shop door. But what a Mr Cole and what a Fanny. He was a tall, stout foreigner, about thirty years of age, ready with tucked-up shirtsleeves and athletic arms to bear my boxes aloft; she was the comeliest of young matrons, her whole face one smile, her ears adorned by weighty gold pendents, and with an obvious twin baby borne in each arm. Husband and wife alike addressed me as 'Meess', and displayed teeth of an enviable regularity and whiteness as they smiled or spoke. Thus much I saw at a first glance.

Too tired for curiosity, I toiled up the narrow staircase after my boxes, washed my dusty face and hot hands, and stepped into my little sitting room, intending to lie down on the sofa and wait as patiently as might be whilst tea, which I had already ordered, was got ready. A pleasant surprise met me. I suppose the good-natured porter may have forewarned Mr Cole of my weakness and wants; be this as it may, there stood the tea ready-brewed, and flanked by pats of butter, small rolls, a rasher, and three eggs wrapped up in a clean napkin. After this, my crowning pleasure for the day was to step into a bed soft as down could make it, and drop to sleep between sheets fragrant of lavender.

A few days' convalescence at H*** did more for me than as many weeks' convalescence in London had effected. Soon I strolled about the beach without numbering the breakwaters, or along the country roads, taking no count of the milestones; and went home to meals as hungry as a schoolgirl, and slept at nights like a baby. One of my earliest street-discoveries was that my landlord's name, as inscribed over his window, was not Cole, but Cola (Nicola) Piccirillo; and a very brief sojourn under his roof instructed me that the Fanny of my friend the porter was called Vanna (Giovanna) by her husband. They were both Neapolitans of the ex-kingdom, though not of the city, of Naples; whenever I asked either of them after the name of their native place, they invariably answered me in a tone of endearment, by what sounded more like '*Vascitammò*'[24] than aught else I know how to spell; but when my English tongue uttered '*Vascitammò*' after them, they would shake their heads and repeat the uncatchable word; at last it grew to be a standing joke between us that, when I became a millionnaire, my courier Cola and my maid Vanna should take the twins and me to see *Vascitammò*.

I never thought of changing my lodgings, though, as time went on, it would have been easy to do so, and certainly the quarter we inhabited was not fashionable. A laborious, not an idle, community environed our doors and furnished customers to the shop: it was some time before I discovered that *l'amico* Piccirillo held a store for polished stones and marine curiosities in the bazaar of H***. He liked to be styled an optician; but whilst he sold and repaired spectacles, driving a prosperous trade amongst the fishing population who surrounded us, and supplying them with cheap telescopes, compasses, and an occasional magic lantern, he was not too proud to eke out his gains by picking up and preparing marine oddities, pebbles, or weeds. After we became intimate, I more than once rose at three or four in the morning, as the turn of the tide dictated, and accompanied him on a ramble of exploration. He scrambled about slippery, jagged rocks as sure-footed as a wild goat; and if ever my climbing powers failed at some critical pass, thought nothing of lifting me over the difficulty, with that courteous familiarity which, in an Italian, does not cease to be re-spectful. I was rather lucky in spying eligible stones, which I con-tributed to his basket; and then, when we got home, he would point out to his wife what *la Signora* had found *'per noi due e per li piccini'*.[25] I understood a little Italian, and they a little English, so we generally, in spite of the Neapolitan blurring accent, made out each other's meaning.

Vanna was one of the prettiest women I ever saw, if indeed I ought to term merely pretty a face which, with good features, contained eyes softer and more lustrous than any others I remember; their colour I never made out, but when she lowered the large eyelids, their long black lashes seemed to throw half her face into shadow. I don't know that she was clever except as a housewife, but in this capacity she excelled, and was a dainty cook over her shining pots and pans: her husband's *'due maccheroni'*[26] often set me hankering, as I spied them done to a turn and smoking hot; though I confess that when Cola brought home a cuttlefish and I saw it dished up as a *'calamarello'*[27] my English prejudice asserted itself.

'Mr and Mrs Cole' were unique in my small experience of people, but surely the twins must have remained unique in anybody's experience. What other babies were ever so fat or so merry? To see their creased arms was enough till one saw their creased legs, and then their arms grew commonplace. I never once heard them cry: a clothes basket formed their primitive bassinette, and there they would sprawl, tickling each other and chuckling. They chuckled at their father, mother, myself, or any stranger who would toss them, or poke a finger into their cushions of fat. They crowed over their own teething, and before they could speak seemed to bandy intuitive jokes, and chuckled in concert. Well were they named Felice Maria and Maria Gioconda.[28] At first sight, they were utterly indistinguishable apart; but experiment proved that Felice was a trifle heavier than his sister, and that fingers could go a hair's-breadth further round her fat waist than round his. When I made their acquaintance, their heads were thickly plaistered with that scurf which apparently an Italian custom leaves undisturbed; but as this wore off, curly black down took its place, and balanced the large, dark eyes and silky eyebrows and lashes which both inherited from their mother. What we, in our insularity, term the English love of soap and water was shared by Vanna, and it was one of my amusements to see the twins in their tub. Often, if hastily summoned to serve behind the counter, Vanna would leave them in the tub to splash about, and throw each other down and pick each other up for a quarter of an hour together; and if I hinted that this might not be perfectly safe for them, she invariably assured me that in her *paese*[29] all the babies toddled about the shore, and into the sea and out again so soon as ever they could toddle. '*E che male vi potrebb'essere? non vi son coccodrilli*'[30] – an argument no less apposite to the tub than to the sea.

As I possessed a small competence and no near home-ties, I felt under no constraint to leave H*** sooner than suited my humour; so, though I had originally intended to remain there no longer than seven or eight weeks, month after month slipped away till a whole year had elapsed, and found me there still. In a year one becomes thoroughly acquainted with daily associates, and from being prepossessed by their engaging aspect, I had come to love and respect Piccirillo and his wife. Both were good Catholics, and evinced their orthodoxy as well by

74

regularity at mass and confession as by strict uprightness towards customers and kindliness towards neighbours. Once, when a fishing boat was lost at sea, and its owner, Ned Gough, left well-nigh penniless, Cola, who was ingenious in preparing marine oddities, arranged a group of young skate in their quaint hoods and mantles, and mounted them on a green board amongst seaweed bushes as a party of gypsies; this would have been raffled for, and the proceeds given to the ruined boatman, had I not taken a fancy to the group and purchased it. And the first time the twins walked out alone was when they crossed over the road hand in hand, each holding an orange as a present to a little sick girl opposite. Both parents watched them safe over, and I heard one remark to the other, that '*Nossignore*'[31] would bless them.

It was mid-May when I arrived at H***, and about mid-May of the year following I returned to London. A legal question had meanwhile arisen touching my small property; and this took so long to settle that during many and many months I remained in doubt whether I should continue adequately provided for, or be reduced to work in some department or other for my living. The point was ultimately decided in my favour, but not before much vexation and expense had been incurred on both sides. At the end of three years from quitting H***, I made up my mind to return and settle there for good: no special ties bound me to London, and I knew no people under whose roof I would so gladly make my solitary home as with Piccirillo and his wife; besides, the twins were an attraction. As to the optician's shop being in an out-of-the-way quarter, that I cared nothing for, having neither the tastes nor the income for fashionable society: so, after a preliminary letter or two had passed between us, I found myself one glowing afternoon in June standing once again on the H*** platform, not in the forlorn position I so vividly remembered, but met by Cola – broader than ever in figure, and smiling his broadest – who whipped up my trunks with his own hands onto the fly and took his place by the driver.

Vanna came running out to meet me at the carriage door, seizing and kissing both my hands; and before I even alighted, two sturdy urchins had been made to kiss *la Signora*'s hand. Ten minutes more and I was seated at tea, chatting to Vanna, and renewing acquaintance with my old friends Felice and Gioconda. This was effected by the presentation to them of a lump of sugar apiece, for which each again kissed my hand, fortunately before their mouths had become sticky by suction.

They were the funniest little creatures imaginable, and two of the prettiest. Felice was still just ahead of Gioconda in bulk, but so much like her that (as I found afterwards), if for fun they exchanged hats, I got into a complete mental muddle as to which was which, confused by the discrepant hats and frocks. There was no paid Roman Catholic school in H***, but the good nuns of St L*** taught the little boys and girls of their congregation; and morning after morning I used to see the twins start for school hand in hand, with dinner as well as books in their bags; for St L*** was too far from their home to admit of going and returning twice in one day. All the neighbours were fond of them; and often, before their destination was reached, a hunch of cake from some good-natured rough hand had found its way into one or other bag, to be shared in due course.

At their books they were '*proprio maravigliosi*',[32] as Vanna phrased it; whilst Cola, swelling with paternal pride under a veil of humility, would observe, '*Non c'è male, nè lui nè lei.*'[33] I believe they really were clever children and fond of their books: at any rate, one Holy Innocents' Day they brought home a prize, a little story in two volumes, one volume apiece; for, as the kind nuns had remarked, they were like one work in two volumes themselves, and should have one book between them. That night they went to bed and fell asleep hand in hand as usual, but each holding in the other hand a scarlet-bound volume, so proud were they. They were but seven years old, and had never yet slept apart: never yet and, as it turned out, never at all.

The Christmas when this happened was one of the brightest and pleasantest I recollect; night after night slight frost visited us, but day after day it melted away, whilst sea and sky spread clear and blue in the sunshine. In other countries much snow had fallen and was still falling, but snow had not yet reached our shores.

Christmas, as usual, brought a few bills to me, and likewise to my friends. Of theirs the heaviest was the Doctor's bill, for the twins had caught scarlatina in the summer, and had got well on a variety of pills and draughts. Then Cola bethought himself of certain money due to him at a coastguard station not many miles from H***, and which would just suffice to pay the Doctor; and one Saturday, a day or two after Twelfth Day, he took the first afternoon train to E***, this being the nearest point on the line to his destination, and went to look after his debtor, telling Vanna that he might not be back before the latest train came into H***.

So Vanna took her seat behind the counter, and looked up the road towards St L***, watching for her little ones to come racing home from school, for school broke up early on Saturdays. As she sat, she knitted something warm and useful, for she was never idle, and hummed in her low, sweet voice the first words of a Christmas carol. I only know those first words, so pathetic in their devout simplicity:

> '*Tu scendi dalle stelle, O Re del Cielo,*
> *E vieni in una grotta al freddo al gelo:*
> *O Bambino mio divino*
> *Io Ti voglio sempre amar!*
> *O Dio beato*
> *E quanto Ti costò l'avermi amato.*'[34]

She was thus occupied as I crossed the shop on my way upstairs, and whilst I paused to say a word in passing, a young woman, her face swollen with crying, came up, who, almost without stopping, called out: 'O Fanny, Fanny, my three are down with the fever, and I'm running for the Doctor!' and in speaking she was gone.

Sympathetic tears had gathered in Vanna's kind eyes when I looked at her. '*Non hanno padre,*'[35] she said, half-apologetically; and I then recollected who the young woman was, and that her children were worse than fatherless. Poor Maggie Crowe! Deserted by a good-for-nothing husband, she worked hard to keep her little ones out of the workhouse; did charing, took in needlework, went out nursing when she could get a job, and now her three children were 'down with the fever', and she had had to leave them alone in her wretched hovel on the east cliff to run a mile and more into H*** to fetch the parish Doctor. We soon saw her tearing back as she had come, not stopping now to speak.

I went to my room, and looking into my charity-purse found that I could afford five shillings out of it for this poor family, and settled mentally that I would take them round next day after church. At the moment I was feeling tired and disinclined to stir, and I concluded the parish Doctor, who bore a character for kindness, would certainly for that night supply his patients with necessaries.

Just after the clock struck three, I heard a bustle below; the twins had come home and were talking eagerly to their mother in their loud, childish voices. I heard Vanna answer them once or twice; then she spoke continuously, seeming to tell them something, and I heard them both reply, '*Mamma sì.*'[36] A few minutes later I was surprised to see them from my window trotting along the street, but not in the direction from which they had just come, and bearing between them a market-basket, each of them holding it by one handle.

A suspicion of their errand crossed my mind, and I hurried downstairs to warn Vanna that a few snowflakes had already fallen and more hung floating about in the still air. She had noticed this of herself, but replied that they knew their way quite well, and it was not far to go; indeed, she could not feel easy without sending up a few oranges left from Twelfth Day for the sick children. Her own had had the fever, they had promised her to go straight and return straight without loitering, and though she looked somewhat anxious she concluded bravely: '*Nossignore avrà cura di loro.*'[37]

I went back to my room thoroughly mortified at the rebuke which her alacrity administered to my laziness. How much less would it not have cost me to set off at once with my five shillings than it cost poor Vanna to send her little ones, tired as perhaps they were, to what, for such short legs, was a considerable distance. From my window, more-over, I soon could not help perceiving that not only the snow, rare at first, had begun to fall rapidly and in large flakes, but that the sky lowered dense and ominous over the east cliff. I felt sure that there – and thither it was that the twins were bound – it must already be snowing heavily.

Four o'clock struck, but Felice and Gioconda had not come back. I heard Vanna closing the shop. In another five minutes she came up to me dressed in bonnet and shawl, with a pale face that told its own story of alarm. Still she would not acknowledge herself frightened, but tried to laugh, as she apologised for leaving me alone in the house, assured me that no one could possibly be calling at that hour, and protested that she would not be out long. If the twins arrived in her absence she was sure I would kindly let them sit by my fire till her return; then, fairly breaking down and crying, she left me, repeating, '*Non son che piccini, poveri piccini, poveri piccini miei.*'[38]

A couple of men with lighted lanterns stood waiting for her in the street; one of them made her take his arm, and I knew by the voice that it was Ned Gough. Hour after hour struck, and they did not return.

About seven o'clock I heard a loud knocking; and running down to open the door – for being left alone in the house I had locked up and made all safe – I found Piccirillo, who on account of the snow had hastened home by an earlier train than he had mentioned, and was now much amazed at finding the house closed and no light burning below. When he understood what had happened, he seemed beside himself with agitation and terror. Flinging up his arms, he rushed from the house, calling out, '*Vanna, Vanna mia! Dove sei? Rispondimi: figli miei, rispondetemi.*'[39] Neighbours came about him, offering what comfort they could think of: but what comfort could there be? He, too, must set off in the snow to seek his poor lost babies and their mother; and soon he started, lantern and stick in hand, ejaculating, and making vows as he went. '*Dio mio, Dio mio, abbi pietà di noi.*'[40]

All through the long night it snowed and snowed: at daybreak it was snowing still. Soon after daybreak the seekers returned, cold, silent, haggard; Piccirillo carrying his wife, who lay insensible in his arms. After hours of wandering they had met somewhere out towards the east cliff, and Vanna, at sight of her husband, had dropped down utterly spent. She had gone straight to Maggie Crowe's cottage, and found that the twins had safely left the oranges there and started homewards; Felice tired but manful, poor little Gioconda trudging wearily along, and clinging to her brother. Maggie had tried to keep them at the cottage as it was already snowing heavily, and the little girl had cried and wanted to stay and warm herself; but her brother said, 'No' – they had promised not to loiter, his sister would be good and not cry, he would take care of her; so whilst Maggie was busy with her own sick children, the twins had started. Beyond this, not one of the searching party could trace them; the small footmarks must have been effaced almost as soon as imprinted on the snow; and any one of the surface inequalities of that snow-waste, which now stretched right and left for miles, might be the mound to cover two such feeble wayfarers.

For three days the frost held and our suspense lasted; then the wind veered from north round to west, a rapid thaw set in, and a few hours ended hope and fear alike. The twins were found huddled together in a chalky hollow close to the edge of the cliff, and almost within sight of Maggie's hovel: Gioconda with her head thrust into the market-basket, Felice with one arm holding the basket over his sister, and with the other clasping her close to him. Her fat hands met round his waist, and clasped between them was a small silver cross I had given her at Christmas, and which she had worn round her neck.

Lovely and pleasant in their lives, in their death they were not divided; but as they had always shared one bed, they now shared one coffin and one grave.

After a while Piccirillo and his wife recovered from their passionate grief; but Vanna drooped more and more as spring came on, and clothed the small grave with greenness. They had no other child, and the house was silent indeed and desolate. Once I heard them talking to each other of *Vascitammò* – Vanna said something I did not catch, and then Cola answered her, '*Sì, Vanna mia, ritorneremo; tolga Iddio che io perda te ancora.*'[41]

So I knew that we should soon have to part. They came upstairs together to me one evening, and with real kindliness explained that all their plans were altered on account of Vanna's failing health, and that they must go home to their own country lest she should die. Vanna cried and I cried, and poor Cola fairly cried too. I promised them that the little grave shall never fall into neglect whilst I live, and in thanking me they managed to say through their tears – '*Nossignore è buono, e certo li avrà benedetti.*'[42]

The business was easily disposed of, for though small, it was a thriving concern, and capable of extension. Other affairs did not take long to settle; and one morning I saw my kind friends off by an early train, on their road through London to *Vascitammò*, which now neither the twins nor I shall ever see.

Pros and Cons

'But, my dear Doctor,' cried Mrs Plume, 'you never can seriously mean it.'

The scene was the Rectory drawing room – teatime; some dozen parishioners drinking tea with their Rector and his wife. Mrs Goodman looked down; her husband, the Rector, looked up.

'I really did mean it,' said he, courteously; 'and, with your permission, I mean it still. Let us consider the matter calmly, my dear Mrs Plume, calmly and fairly; and to start us fairly I will restate my proposal, which is that we should all combine to do our best towards bringing about the abolition of pews from our parish church.'

'Then I,' returned Mrs Plume, shaking her head airily, 'must really restate my protest. You never seriously can mean it.'

'Nay,' resumed the Rector, 'don't think that I am unmindful of your feelings on this point' – and he glanced round the circle. 'If I spoke hastily, I ask your pardon and patience; but this matter of pews and pew-rents is on my conscience, and *that* I must lighten at all costs; even, Mr Sale' – for Mr Sale frowned – 'at the cost of my income. However, why should we conclude ourselves to be at variance before we have ventilated the matter in hand? I for one will never take for granted that any good Christian is against the acknowledgement of our absolute equality before God.'

'Sir,' interposed Mr Blackman, 'we are equals, whatever may be our colour or our country. But whilst the Zenana counts its victims by thousands, whilst the Japanese make boast of their happy despatch, whilst the Bushman, dwindling before our face, lives and dies as the beasts that perish, shall we divert our attention from such matters of life and death to fix it on a petty question of appearance? Pardon me if tears for our benighted brethren blind me to such a matter as this.'

'Our benighted brethren,' said the Rector, gravely, 'have my pity, have my prayers, have my money in some measure. Of your larger gifts in these several kinds I will not ask you to divert one throb, or one word, or one penny in favour of our poor fellow-parishioners. No, dear friend, help us by your good example to enlarge our field of charitable labour; to stretch full-handed towards remote spots; but not meanwhile to fail in breaking up our own fallow ground at home. We all know that if at this moment either our foreign or our native ragged brother were to present himself in church, however open our hearts may be to him, our pew-doors would infallibly be shut against him, and he would find himself looked down upon both literally and figuratively. This, I own to you, were I he, would discomfit me, and put a stumbling block in my way as a worshipper.'

'Pooh! pooh!' broke in Mr Wood, testily. 'My dear fellow, I really thought you a wiser man. What hardship is it for a flunky or a clod-hopper to sit in a seat without a door?'

'Ah!' rejoined the Rector quietly, 'for a servant, as you say, or for a mere sower of our fields, or (why not?) for a carpenter's son either? But allow me to name two points which strike me forcibly – two very solemn points' – and Dr Goodman spoke with solemnity, and bowed his head. 'First, that if our adorable Lord were now walking this world as once He walked it, and if He had gone into our parish church last Sunday – as long ago He used to frequent the synagogue of Nazareth – He would certainly not have waited long to be ushered into a pew, but would, at least as willingly, have sat down amongst His own "blessed" poor; and, secondly, that we should all have left Him to do so un-molested; for I cannot suppose that His were the gold ring and goodly apparel which would have challenged attention.'

There was a pause, broken by Mrs Plume, who, turning to her hostess, observed: 'Ah, dear Mrs Goodman, we know and revere the zeal of our dear good apostle. But you and I are old housekeepers, old birds not to be caught with chaff ' – and she shook a fascinating finger at her pastor – 'and we know that the poor are not nice neighbours; quite infectious, in fact. They do very well together all in a clump, but one really couldn't risk sitting amongst them, on various grounds, you know.'

'Well,' resumed the Rector, 'I plead guilty to being but a tough man, thick-skinned, and lacking certain subtler members, entitled nerves. But what will you? You must make allowances for me, and even put up with me as I am. With docility, and all the imagination of which I am master, I throw myself into your position, and shudder with you at these repulsively infectious poor. I even seek to deepen my first impression of horror by questioning myself in detail, and I dwell on the word "infectious". This brings before me smallpox, typhus fever, and other dreadful ailments; and I hasten (in spirit) to slam to, if only I could to bolt and bar, my pew-door. Safely ensconced within, I peer over my necessary barrier, and, relieved from the pressure of instant peril, gaze with pity on the crowd without, all alike typhus-stricken, all alike redolent of smallpox. A new terror thrills me. Are "all alike" infectious? or have we grouped together sound and unsound, sick and healthy? Ah, you hint, that amount of risk cannot be helped if they are to come to church at all. I am corrected, and carrying out the lesson of my Teacher I echo: that amount of risk cannot be helped if we are to come to church at all.'

'These men! these men!' cried Mrs Plume, gaily. And Miss Crabb observed, from behind her blue spectacles, 'Well, I suppose a woman of my age may allude to anything she pleases; so I make bold to tell you, Dr Goodman, that smallpox may be all nonsense; but that nobody would like to sit amongst smells, and cheek by jowl with more heads than one in a bonnet.'

'Smells,' rejoined the Rector, 'I do strongly object to; including scents, my dear Mrs Plume; but that is a matter of taste. The other detail, which I know not how to express more pointedly than in the striking words of Miss Crabb, is yet more to be deprecated: but let us consider whether pews fairly meet the difficulty. Fairly? I ask – and then unhesitatingly answer, "No." For all the poor, both clean and dirty, occupy our free seats together; and surely to sit next a dirty neighbour is, at the least, as great a hardship on the cleanly poor as it would be on the rich, who are so far better able to have their clothes cleansed, or even, in case of need, to discard them. If, indeed, all dirty individuals would have the good feeling to compact themselves into one body, it might be reassuring to their fellows, but this it were invidious to propose; and besides, we are at present mooting pews or no pews, not any third possible – or shall we say impossible? – alternative. I confess to you,' he resumed, very seriously, 'when I remember the little stress laid by Christ on clean hands, and the paramount importance in His eyes of a clean heart; when I reflect on the dirt of all kinds which must have touched Him in the crowds He taught and healed; when I realise that every one of my parishioners, poor as well as rich, will confront me at His judgement-bar, I tremble lest any should be deterred from coming to Him because I am too fine a gentleman to go out into the highways and hedges, and compel to come in those actual poor – foul of body, it may be, as well as of soul – whom yet He has numbered to me as my flock.'

Silence ensued – an uncomfortable silence; broken by Mrs Goodman's nervous proffer of tea to Mr Sale, who declined it.

Mr Home resumed the attack. 'Doctor,' observed he, 'all other objections to open seats might perhaps be overruled; but consider the sacredness of family affection, and do not ask us to scatter ourselves forlornly through the church, here a husband, there a wife' – and he interchanged a smile with Mrs Home – 'there, again, a practical orphan. I for one could not possibly say my prayers without my little woman at my elbow.'

'Here,' cried the Rector, 'I joyfully meet you halfway. The division of the sexes in distinct aisles is a question by itself, and one which I am not now discussing. Only go betimes to church' – at this a glance of intelligence passed round the circle, whilst Mrs Home coloured – 'and I stake my credit that you will hardly ever fail to find six contiguous seats for your party.'

Then Mr Stone spoke up – Mr Stone, the warmest man in the parish. He spoke with his fat hands in his fat pockets.

'Dr Goodman, sir' – the courteous Rector bowed – 'my attachment to the Church and my respect for your cloth must not prevent my doing my duty by my fellow-parishioners, whose mouthpiece on the present occasion I claim to be.' A general movement of relief accepted him as the lay champion. 'We acknowledge, sir, and appreciate your zeal amongst us, but we protest against your innovations. We have borne with chants, with a surpliced choir, with daily services, but we will not bear to see all our rights trampled under foot, and all our time-hallowed usages set at nought. The tendency of the day is to level social distinctions and to elevate unduly the lower orders. In this parish at least let us combine to keep up wise barriers between class and class, and to maintain that fundamental principle practically bowed to all over our happy England – that what you can pay for you can purchase. This, sir, has been our first dissension' – a statement not quite correct – 'let it be our last; and in token that we are at one again, here is my hand.'

Dr Goodman grasped the proffered hand, looking rather pale as he did so.

'Let this betoken,' rejoined he, 'that whatever is discarded amongst us, it shall not be Christian charity. And now it grows late. I must not selfishly prolong our discussion; yet, as your pastor, with a sacred duty to discharge towards all my flock, suffer me to add one word. What Mr Stone has alleged may be the system of worldly England; though many a man professing far less than we do would repudiate so monstrous a principle; but as Churchmen we can have nothing to do with it. God's gifts are bought without money and without price: "Ho, everyone," cries His invitation. I, therefore, as His most unworthy ambassador, protest that in His house I will no longer buy and sell as in a market. I confess myself in fault that I have so long tolerated this monstrous abuse; and I avow that you, my brethren, have this evening furnished me with the only plausible argument in favour of pews which has ever been suggested to me, for it *is* hard upon our open-hearted poor that they should be compelled to sit by persons who, instead of viewing them as brethren beloved, despise the poor.'

The Waves of This Troublesome World

1

Perhaps there is no pleasanter watering place in England where to spend the fine summer months than Hastings, on the Sussex coast. The old town, nestling in a long, narrow valley, flanked by the east and west hills, looks down upon the sea. At the valley mouth, on the shingly beach, stands the fish-market, where boatmen disembark the fruit of daily toil; where traffic is briskly plied, and maybe haggling rages; where bare-legged children dodge in and out between the stalls; where now and then a travelling show – dwarf, giant, or what not – arrests for brief days its wanderings.

Hard by the market, on the beach, stands the fishermen's chapel – plain but comely, with, near the door, its small chest for offerings. I know not whether chanted psalms and hymns rise within its walls; but if they do, the windy sea must sound an accompaniment exceeding in solemn harmony any played upon earthly organs, to such words as, 'One deep calleth another, because of the noise of the water-pipes: all Thy waves and storms are gone over me,' or, 'They are carried up to the heaven, and down again to the deep: their soul melteth away because of the trouble,' or, 'Let not the water-flood drown me, neither let the deep swallow me up.'

It is a pretty sight in brilliant holiday weather to watch the many parties of health- or pleasure-seekers which throng the beach. Boys and girls picking up shells, pebbles and starfishes, or raising with hands and wooden spades a sand fortress, encircled by a moat full of seawater, and crowned by a twig of seaweed as a flag; mothers and elder sisters reading or working beneath shady hats, whilst after bathing their long hair dries in the sun and wind. Hard by rock at their moorings bannered pleasure-boats, with blue-jerseyed oarsmen or white sails; and if the weather is oppressively hot and sunny, a gaily coloured canopy is reared on light poles, for the protection of voyagers. When tide is high, a plank or a long step suffices; but at low water, as the shore is flat, boatmen have frequently to carry children, and even women, across the broad stretch of wet sands to and from vessels.

Very different from such seafarers in sport are their near neighbours, the seafarers in earnest, who neither hoist canopies for fair weather, nor tarry at home for foul; who might say with the patriarch Jacob, 'In the day the drought consumed me, and the frost by night'; whose vigils often see the moon rise and set; who sometimes buffet with the winds and tug against the tide for very life.

It is with one of these that my tale has to do: let us peep into his cottage.

An accident to his boat – only just now, after hours of diligent labour – repaired, has kept Frank Hardiman on shore all day. Within another hour the tide will be favourable, and he must be put to sea; till then he stays with his wife and two children, Jane and Henry. They are seated at tea, discussing the contents of a letter received that afternoon. Let us look at the faces and listen to the conversation.

Frank Hardiman is thirty-one years old, tall, stout, tanned by the sun, with a deep, jolly voice, bright eyes, and the merriest of laughs. His wife, Emma, is slim and rather pretty, dressed with considerable taste and uncommon neatness; for before her marriage she was upper nurse in a gentleman's family, and indeed made acquaintance with her good man when loitering along the beach after her little charges. Jane is nine years old, quiet and shy, with a mild expression, redeemed from insipidity by lines of unusual firmness about the mouth: when she speaks, it is mostly in a slow, apathetic manner; but now and then a flash of feeling reveals that there are strength and depth in her character. Harry has scarcely entered his seventh year, and is a miniature likeness of his father, only less sunburnt.

The letter under discussion ran as follows:

Dear brother and sister,

My husband died ten days ago in the hope of a blessed resurrection. Moreover God, Who does all things well, has been pleased to call my sin to remembrance, and to slay my son. I am alone indeed now; not in debt, having just enough in hand to pay my way till Thursday, and then come down to you. Will you receive me? We parted in anger, but perhaps you will forgive me when you know how much I have lost, and guess with how sore a longing I desire to lay my bones amongst my own people. If I do not hear from you by Thursday, I shall understand that you cannot forgive: nevertheless remember, in the next world if not in this, we must meet again.

Your sorrowful, affectionate sister,
– Sarah Lane

'How can she fancy we'd bear malice after all her troubles?' said Frank; 'and when it was for her own good, too. Write at once, my dear, and make her welcome to all we've got, such as it is, and the best of it.'

'Yes,' replied Emma, drily. She was jealously alive to her husband's fondness for his sister, and by no means relished the prospect of her returning to live with them.

'How old is Aunt Sarah?' enquired Jane.

'Twenty-five last March; and five years ago she was the prettiest girl in Hastings. You must furbish up your room a bit, Jenny, and make your aunt as comfortable as you can. She's got rather high notions, naturally; but I guess they must have come down by this time, poor thing! Only don't let us make her feel strange coming back to what used to be her home – and shall be her home again, please God, if she'll come and share it. Well, I'm off, Emma,' continued Frank, rising and shaking himself: 'you'll write a kind welcome, I know, for you're the scholar; and you needn't say a word about me, except that I'm just the same as five years ago. Good night.' – 'Good night.' So he left the cottage.

Then Jane busied herself with washing the tea things and 'tidying up' – Harry, at the imminent risk of his fingers, began hacking a small bit of wood, to produce what he dubbed a boat, and Emma sat down to write the letter of invitation – I cannot say welcome:

My dear Sister,

Your letter came to hand this afternoon, and Frank and I are very sorry for your troubles; but if you come here I dare say you will mind less. Frank says, 'Come and welcome, and be as all was five years ago' – only ours is but a poor place for such as you, and you must not mind having Jenny in bed with you; and you cannot expect me to do nothing but wait on you, as I have a good handful with Frank and the children, I tell you plainly.

So next Thursday we shall expect you, and no more at present from

Your affectionate sister,

– Emma Hardiman

Whilst Emma wrote her letter, Jane, I say, washed the tea things. There was brisk thoroughness in her manner of washing; no great handiness, but concentrated energy: she was evidently conscientious. Next she coaxed Harry to forego his hacking and be put to bed, showing tact and good nature with firmness in the transaction. Then, returning with her bonnet on her head and a basket on her arm, she asked her mother whether she should not take her letter to the post.

'Yes,' answered Emma; 'and you must make haste, too, or it won't be in time. Here's a penny for a stamp; and' – putting a crown-piece into the little girl's hand – 'you must bring me in some butter, and sugar, and treacle, and a loaf, and some tea; and call at Mrs Smith's for my bonnet, and get a reel of black cotton and a paper of needles. And you must run, too; you'll have running enough, I reckon, when madam comes.'

Away ran Jane with all her might, reaching the post office in much more than time to catch the evening mail. 'Well, my little woman, is it a love letter you're carrying?' said the postmaster; to which she answered demurely, 'No, sir, please; it's to my aunt in London.' Seeing he was busy, she added no more, but set off on her next errand. This took her to a various-smelling shop in one of the backstreets, where she ran glibly through the accustomed list of articles: 'Half a pound of butter, a pound of sugar, two pennyworth of treacle (for Harry), a quartern loaf, a quarter of a pound of three-and-fourpenny tea, and two rashers of bacon,' supplying the last item from her knowledge of what must be wanted, though her mother had forgotten to name it. She packed all carefully in her little basket, counted the change from her crown-piece, chirped to a poor imprisoned lark, which could catch not one glimpse of sky from his nail in the shop, stroked her old friend the black cat, and started for Mrs Smith's smart establishment in the High Street.

Mrs Smith, in a false front and staring flowers, presiding behind her millinery counter, looked somewhat formidable. Jane preferred asking the young woman on the other side for the black cotton and needles. These were supplied and paid for; then Mrs Smith called out to know if she wanted anything else. 'Please, ma'am,' began Jane, 'is mother's bonnet –'

'Oh!' cried Mrs Smith, shortly, 'tell your mother that her bonnet isn't done yet, and she needn't keep bothering after it; for when it's done I'll send it home, and not before. Good evening!' This bonnet was a bone of contention between the two women: it was to be trimmed in return for certain errands already executed by Jane; and the milliner's hands being filled just now with more lucrative orders, great delay ensued in its completion.

When Jane reached home, she found her mother seated hard at work making a black-and-white muslin dress with flounces – Emma loved to be smart on Sunday – for her own wear. Jane put away the purchases, handed what change remained to Mrs Hardiman, and sat down to write a copy and work an addition sum for Mrs Grey, the curate's wife, who gave her an hour's instruction two or three times a week. The little girl laboured to do her very best, and had just produced a particularly correct capital B when her mother shook the table. Not a word said poor Jane, though a great blot was jerked out of the pen onto the B. She tried again and again for six lines more, but without equalling the defaced B; then, that page finished, turned her mind to the sum. '4 and 4 are 8, and 1 are 9, and 7 –' 'Jane,' cried her mother, 'there's nothing for supper; run out and fetch two rashers.' 'I got them, Mother, when I was out, because I knew they were wanted,' was the cheerful answer, and reckoning recommenced. '4 and 4 are 8, and 1 are 9, and 7 are sixt—' 'Jane.' 'Yes, Mother.' 'Was the letter in time?' 'Oh, much more than time. 4 and 4 –' 'I shall never get through these flounces tonight: put away your books, child, and help me. I'm sure your schooling isn't worth much if it doesn't teach you to mind me.'

Jane jumped up, though she could have cried, laid by her book and slate, and sat down close to her mother. In another minute two pairs of hands were hemming as fast as they could hem at the flounces. Why was Emma in such a hurry to finish making her dress? It could not be out of regard to her sister-in-law's feelings, as she and her daughter were already in black for the death of an old relation who had left them a few pounds; neither could it be with an exclusive eye to Sunday, for this was only Tuesday evening: no, she was bent on receiving poor, sad Sarah in this fine gown, because she felt jealous of her good looks, and wanted to outshine her in Frank's eyes.

Jane, who had no idea of this state of things, asked, 'What was Uncle Lane?'

'Don't call him uncle,' returned Emma, sharply; 'he was no kith or kin to us, but a Methodist photographer, and but a poor body at best. I dare say his widow hasn't a pound that she can call her own, though she is so ready to invite herself to live with them who work hard for their bread. However, your father must please himself ' – the thread snapped – 'Mrs Smith's cotton is mere rubbish; you go to Widow Wright's next time, and see if you can't get an honest penn'orth; do you hear?'

'Yes, Mother. I shall like to have Aunt Sarah in my bed: is she like father?'

'No – yes – I don't know; don't bother me. You'll have enough and to spare of Aunt Sarah, I can tell you.'

Silence once more, except for the click, click of thimble and needle; Jane wondering what she had said amiss, for her mother was not usually cross.

At last the flounces were finished. 'There, that will do,' observed Emma, more complacently, for they looked puffy and well. 'I declare it's supper-time; make haste, child, and toast the bacon whilst I clear away.'

On Wednesday Jane – having, under her mother's direction, scrubbed her own bedroom floor – added a blue basin and jug to its furniture, and an extra chair. The window looked into Frank's garden, very bright just now with nasturtiums; and though it did not command a sea view, the murmur, or tumult, or roar of the great deep, could always, except in very still weather, be distinctly heard from it.

The room made ready, let us glance at its future occupant.

Sarah Lane, now so mournful, had years ago been not only the prettiest, but almost the merriest girl in Hastings. True, she was a child of sorrow to her mother, who died without even kissing her newborn baby; but, bequeathed to the guardianship of father and brother, she never missed a mother's care. Often might Henry Hardiman be seen loitering up and down the parade, or lounging by the sundial, holding in his arms his little girl; or, as she grew older, putting his finger into her chubby fist to help her in toddling. Sometimes, in pleasant weather, he took her in the boat with him for a row; sometimes left her on shore under the care of Frank, who lugged her unweariedly about the beach, where she served as plaything to her father's rugged mates.

When the time arrived for Frank to go out with his father and share his labours, a change ensued for little Sarah. She was sent to a superior school – for Henry Hardiman drove a flourishing trade – and only went home on a Saturday to stay till the Monday – the Hardimans, from father to son, observing Sunday and frequenting St Clement's Church. Henry and Frank were not a little proud of their girl as she walked beside them, rosy and good-humoured, or, with a pretty childish voice, joined in the hymns of the congregation; and before long she, too, learnt to be proud of her sturdy, weather-beaten father in his Sunday blue coat, and of her handsome, merry brother, and to give them back warm love for the lifelong love which they gave her.

At fifteen, grown tall and womanly, Sarah came home to keep her father's house. Her school-education included several useful items: she was quick and clever with her needle, read with fluency and expression, wrote a clear hand, was a capital accountant, had a fair knowledge of geography, history, and spelling, could express herself well in a letter; moreover, she knew a little music and a little dancing, and, thanks to natural voice and ear, sang sweetly and tuneably. Very soon the cottage bore witness to her good taste. The old-fashioned furniture was rubbed up; a few geraniums and fuchsias screened the parlour window; a Virginia creeper, scarlet-coloured in autumn, clambered up the outer wall; and carefully tended plants rendered her garden the prettiest in the Tackle Way. She liked and wore bright colours; and when she watered her window-flowers, or gathered a nosegay in the garden, or sat among the Pier Rocks watching for her father's boat to come across the intense blue, sunny sea, often and often passers-by lingered to admire her noble beauty and untaught grace.

When her skill as a needlewoman became known, first neighbours, then ladies engaged her to work for them. By this means she amassed a little sum of money, carefully stored amongst her treasures, but never spent. Sometimes Henry, coming home, found her sewing and singing, whilst puss purred at her feet, and the kettle sang on the fire. Then he would say, 'Bless you, Sally; there's no need for you to wear out your plump bits of fingers. Ain't Frank and I big enough to work for you?' And she would answer, 'Ah, but some day when you're a dear old father, and stay at home in the chimney corner, Frank mustn't have all the pleasure of working for you, and my earnings will come in handy, you'll see.'

Several young men courted her for her fair face, or clever ways, or kind heart; but to all of them she answered a civil 'no,' till it came to be said among the fisherfolk that Sarah Hardiman must be waiting for a lord. Even John Archer, a well-to-do, God-fearing young boatman, who followed her for many an anxious month, only at last elicited her gentle, firm 'no,' though her father pitied the poor lad, and Frank spoke warmly in his favour. Soon after Sarah left school, Frank married and brought home his Emma; but Sarah continued mistress of the house, her father's darling, and very dear to her brother, which, with her good looks and many suitors, made Emma sore and jealous. The two young women were not over-cordial together, though they never spoke of their coolness, and Frank was long before he even suspected it.

So four years passed.

One Saturday night, as the little family sat round the fire, over which spluttered eggs and bacon for supper – as Henry dozed, Frank netted, Emma worked for her baby, and Sarah turned the rashers – a noise of quarrelling outside roused the two men. They started up, but before they could reach the door a loud crash was heard of something falling and breaking on the pavement; then three or four voices cried, 'Shame!' They ran out, and the women were left alone in some anxiety.

After a few minutes old Hardiman returned. 'Sally,' explained he, 'here's a poor travelling showman whose box of things has just been smashed by big Ben, because he said the sun would take his likeness. Ben, I reckon, has had a glass too much. So I think it will be but Christian-like to take him in for tonight, as he's quite a stranger here, and seems a decent body, if you'll shake him down a bed, my darling.'

'Yes, father,' answered the girl; and just then Frank and a young man entered, bearing between them the wrecks of a portable photographic apparatus.

'Sit down and be kindly welcome,' Sarah said, blushing like a rose; she set a chair for the stranger and, with practical hospitality, broke three more eggs, and put three more rashers into the frying pan. Then she placed those already cooked on the table, with cheese, butter, home-made bread and strong beer.

At supper the guest warmly thanked his entertainers, and proceeded to gratify their curiosity about himself. His name was John Lane; both his parents were dead and, indeed, he had no near relation in the world. His business was to take photographs, at sixpence and upwards; for this purpose he travelled from town to town, seldom remaining in one place for more than a few weeks: 'Till tonight,' he continued, somewhat bitterly, 'I never met with an ignorant brute.' He then drew from his pocket a small case containing specimens of his art, both portraits and landscapes.

Frank looked at them in silent admiration; but Sarah observed, pointing to a coloured head, 'I like that best; I always want to know what eyes and hair people have.' John Lane glanced up at her: 'Yes,' said he, 'the sun can't paint eyes and hair.' 'Well, Mr Lane,' interposed Emma, 'I must get you to do Jenny's portrait. When will you be able?' 'I will come as soon as I possibly can,' he answered, eagerly. So that evening concluded.

Next morning, while they sat at breakfast, Sarah said to the guest, 'Our old church is worth seeing: I think when you've been there with us, you'll want to take its likeness too.' But John Lane, flushing crimson, replied, without looking up, 'I can't go there, thank you: I'm what you call a Methodist.'

Certainly John Lane by no means exaggerated in his own favour when he told his story. He might have said that during some years he had been the sole support of a bedridden mother, for her sake often denying himself all save bare necessaries; that by perseverance and ingenuity he had attained proficiency in his art; that he had laid up a sum of money, and was in the way to add to it. Anyone who knew him well could have related these facts and more. Two years before this period, about the time of his mother's death, he stopped one Sunday afternoon to hear an itinerant preacher, who, bareheaded, Bible in hand, went out – to use his own phrase – into the highways and hedges, to compel men to come in. John stopped to kill time; but the rough, zealous words pricked his conscience to the quick: before he went his way he had resolved to redeem the time. From that day he was an altered man: he read his Bible with fervent, persistent prayer, and at the first opportunity introduced himself to the preacher whose words had convinced him of sin. These two men, both honest, both zealous, both uninstructed, provoked each other to good works; but, utterly alien from church unity, ignored many vital doctrines. The elder man, constrained by the love of Christ, sailed as a missionary to India: John Lane then believed that he was called to fill the gap; to lift up his voice like a trumpet, and proclaim the gospel to souls perishing for lack of knowledge. Therefore he gave up his fixed quarters in London, and wandering from town to town, endeavoured to speak a word in season to persons who came to him in the way of business; and on Sundays, after attending one service in the Methodist chapel, devoted his afternoon to out-of-door preaching.

This was the man whom what we call accident – but what is in fact the appointment or permission of God – brought to the fisherman's cottage; to Hardiman and Frank, staunch churchgoers; to Emma, not over-partial to her sister-in-law; to beautiful Sarah, with her winning ways and disengaged heart.

Of course John Lane deemed himself in duty bound to bear witness for the truth here as elsewhere. Hardiman listened to him, but shook his head when he spoke of the love of the Establishment having waxed cold, of experience, and professors. 'I like practisers,' said Henry Hardiman; and trudged to St Clement's as heretofore. Emma went once to the Methodist chapel, but was mightily offended when the preacher – looking, as she declared, full at her light blue bonnet – observed, 'It might have been better for Dives in hell[43] if he had not dressed so finely.' Sarah, who would not grieve her father, continued a regular attendant at the old parish church once every Sunday; but if, as frequently happened, in her afternoon stroll she caught sight of John Lane surrounded by a group of listeners, too often idlers, she was sure to join his audience and add her sweet voice to their hymns. Then followed the walk together home; the earnest communings by the way, of God, and Jesus, and heaven, of the everlasting burnings to be fled from, and the everlasting prize to be run for.

So these two came to love each other: Henry only saw that the young man loved his beautiful daughter.

'John Lane,' said he one day, 'you love Sarah, and mean well by her; but I tell you plainly she's not for such as you. She's said "no" to many a man already, and she'll say "no" to you when you ask her: for she shall never have my blessing on her marrying a Methodist, and gadding from place to place making mischief. Take my advice, my lad, and keep away from Sarah, and she won't run after you.'

So John kept away from the cottage; and if Sarah fretted, she said not a word of her troubles to anyone.

About a week had elapsed since they last saw each other, when she, having finished some work for a lady at Halton, set off to carry it home. A long round led her to the field-path, beset by fence and gates: on the right, where the west hill slopes towards the town, haymaking was going on with a pleasant smell. Scarcely a breath of wind stirred: and when for a few minutes she sat on a wayside bench to cool herself, she noticed how a subtle exhalation rising from the heated ground became perceptible where it slightly altered the appearance of objects seen through it.

Her business at Halton was quickly transacted; and with lightened hands, if not a lightened heart, she was turning homewards, when straight before her, pack on back, stood John Lane.

Sarah looked very tall and stately: 'Goodbye, Mr Lane,' said she, 'since I see you're on your travels again; and I hope you'll find a kinder welcome where you're going than you got at Hastings.'

'Goodbye, indeed,' he answered, gravely, 'if you call me Mr Lane; and I hope I shall never find such another kind welcome, if it's only to break my heart afterwards.'

It was not in human nature to part so: no wonder Sarah's look softened; no wonder John forgot his pack and his migration, and turned back towards Hastings with her. He told her all: how her father had called him a mischief-making Methodist; had said he had no chance, and had better keep away; how he had prayed and wrestled against temptation; 'because,' added he, simply, 'I wasn't sure, Sarah, that you would say "no". But God gave me grace to esteem the reproach of Christ better than all the – ah, better than much more than all the treasures of Egypt.' Again he said, 'Goodbye,' but Sarah said, 'Stuff! You know, John, I can't answer "yes" or "no" till you ask me something.'

So in the field-path John asked, and she answered. Then from gate to gate along the steaming fields, whilst haymakers rested and birds sat silent in the noon heat, they two walked, talking earnestly. At the last gate they parted, Sarah saying, 'Very well, now that's settled. John, I do believe my soul is at stake in this matter, for it's only you in all the world who have taught me to love God; and though father won't bless my marrying a Methodist, he'll bless me when I am married.'

They were married secretly one Sunday morning at the Methodist chapel – not without keen stings of conscience, which neither owned to the other. When that same day Henry Hardiman heard from them what was done, he uttered no angry words, but took the blow stoutly. To his daughter's eager expressions of affection he merely answered, 'Maybe, maybe, Sally,' and when a week later she and her husband set off for Eastbourne, he blessed her gravely before she went.

But that one trouble had made an old man of him. Soon Frank went alone to fish, while Henry sat at home in the chimney corner, holding Emma's youngest born on his knee, or crept along the Tackle Way, with a finger in Jane's chubby fist to help her in toddling. Next, days came when he could only sit moping in the chimney corner: the Doctor, looking at him, shook his head; and Frank wrote Sarah word that if she cared for her father's pardon she must come now and ask it. She came: was received coldly by her brother and sister-in-law, kindly by her father; only when she hung about him with tears and fond words, he answered patiently, 'Maybe, maybe, Sally.' So he died.

A few more months and Sarah became mother of a small, weak baby – a little Henry. A few more years and still wearing black for her dead only son, she sat beside her husband's deathbed: her kind husband, who never once had spoken a harsh word to her. Long ago they had repented of the cruel wrong done to the old man; had confessed their fault one to the other, exchanged forgiveness, and prayed together for pardon. Their store of money wasted during John's tedious illness; and Sarah, watching him as he lay dying, felt a sort of satisfaction in the thought that she had just enough left to bury her dead out of sight before asking help of her relations.

His last look was at her; his last words were, 'Thanks be to God, which giveth us the victory through our Lord Jesus Christ.'

2

Thursday afternoon arrived. Frank, Jane and little Harry went down to the station to meet Sarah Lane; whilst Emma stayed at home in the puffy new muslin, preparing tea and making ready for her sister-in-law's reception. She was in high good humour; for Frank before setting off had praised her pretty face, and observed, 'Poor Sally won't look like that, I fancy, when she comes home again.'

She came. Just the old stately grace and fine features, but none of the old bloom; her eyes were dim and sunken, her cheeks hollow; instead of bright colours she wore widow's weeds. She came back to the familiar home, the fond warm-hearted brother, the sister-in-law who had never loved her; only the dear old man was wanting, whose grey hairs she had brought down with sorrow to the grave.

Frank kissed his sister when she crossed the threshold, but could not utter one word of welcome, struck dumb by her changed face: it was Emma who, really touched, came forward and welcomed her cordially. Not much was said that evening. Sarah held little Henry – so like his grandfather – on her lap till he fell fast asleep there, and Frank carried him upstairs for Jane to put to bed. Then Sarah, left alone with her sister-in-law, rose, and holding out her hand said, 'Emma, I promised John to ask your pardon for the ill will there has been between us, and I do ask it. Please God, I shall not stand in your way any more to vex you, nor eat the bread of idleness for long. Good night.' To judge by her wasted form and frequent hacking cough, she would not for long eat the bread of men at all.

The next day and the next, Sarah went amongst her neighbours seeking for needlework, but without success. Many old friends greeted her coldly, for Henry Hardiman's death was generally laid at her door. Some promised to employ her, but had no work just then. She called at several houses from which she used to receive orders, but her richer customers had not yet left London for the seaside: she trudged to Halton, and found that the young lady who employed her there had married long ago, and gone away to the lake country.

Poor Sarah! She was a widow indeed, and desolate, trusting in God.

On Sunday morning, before setting out for chapel, she said, 'Don't wait dinner for me, as I dare say I shan't be back much before tea-time.' Emma tossed her head in its flowered crape bonnet, and wondered to Frank 'which of her Methodist friends will give her a dinner?'

Sarah Lane sat down to no dinner that day; but when she felt pretty certain that the congregation must have dispersed from St Clement's, she went into the churchyard and sat down on her father's grave. There, motionless, silent, past crying, she remained for hours. Will, mental powers, life itself, seemed at a standstill; whilst, as if of their own accord, old days came back before her eyes. She remembered toddling along, helped by the unwearied finger; being rowed out to sea in pleasant weather, till, grown tired, she nestled to sleep under the rough greatcoat; changing once a week from lessons and school discipline to snug home; walking hand in hand to church. She remembered being installed mistress of the cottage; altering, renewing, embellishing, just as she pleased; being fondled, cared for, scarcely allowed to work for him who toiled night and day for her; continuing first and dearest even after Frank brought a wife to live with them. She remembered the new love that hardened her against the old; the tacit deceit; the short parting, with its blessing, grave and sorrowful; the long, long parting, with its patient, unvaried 'Maybe, maybe, Sally'. Over and over again her eye mechanically read –

HENRY HARDIMAN,
AGED 55.
Affliction sore long time he bore,
Physicians were in vain,
Till God did please his soul release,
And ease him of his pain.

She did not perceive that these lines are doggerel; she only felt that they were true. Her baby, her dear John – their loss seemed light while she sat by her dead father whom she had killed, and heard his feeble voice saying in her ears, 'Maybe, maybe, Sally.'

'My!' cried Emma, when, as the kettle sang on the fire and Jane knelt on the hearth toasting huge slices for tea, Sarah crept into the cottage with a few daisies and blades of grass in her hand: 'you startled me just like a ghost, and I declare you're as white as one.'

It cost Sarah's pride a severe struggle before she could bring herself to apply for work to Mrs Grey, the curate's wife: she feared some harsh word might be dropped concerning her own conduct years ago; and John blamed for what, as she persisted in saying, she led him into. But no employment offered elsewhere; and the words of Holy Scripture, 'If any would not work, neither should he eat', kept goading her; till one afternoon, by a great effort, she set off towards the curate's old-fashioned house in the Croft. A strange servant opened the door, and perceiving a decent-looking widow, led her straight into the sitting room. Mrs Grey heard someone enter but, not catching the name, looked up from her writing, and seeing as she supposed a stranger, rose and enquired civilly to whom she had the pleasure of speaking.

'You don't recollect me, ma'am,' began Sarah; but at the sound of that familiar voice Mrs Grey started forward and, cordially pressing her hand, exclaimed, 'Oh, Sarah Hardiman – Mrs Lane – how glad I am to see you! I heard you were come home, and thought it would not be long before you paid me a visit. Sit down, and let me help you off with your bonnet and shawl; for now you are here I shall not let you go so easily.'

This kindness quite overcame the poor widow. A great flow of tears relieved her; and when Mrs Grey spoke soothing words, she answered, 'Let be, ma'am, let be: it's the first time since I buried John, and it does me good.'

So the curate's wife, who had known her from a baby, seated herself by her; and drawing the bowed-down head to her bosom, let her sob there, not attempting to check her grief, but only whispering that she understood the lightest part of it, having lost her own youngest boy five months ago. When the sobs grew less choking, she poured out a glass of wine and made her eat some cake – little guessing how sorely her guest stood in need of food; since Sarah grudged herself every morsel she ate whilst she earned nothing and was a burden to Frank and Emma.

At length the purpose of her visit was told: 'I came to ask,' said Sarah, 'whether you would give me some needlework. I have been trying ever since I came back to find employment, and no one wants my services. Will you let me work for you?'

Mrs Grey replied directly, 'I have plenty of things to make just now, and you shall have them all if you like to begin tomorrow.' Then, remembering that in days of yore there was not much cordiality between the sisters-in-law, she added, 'If you don't mind, I should prefer your not taking them home, at least not at first, but working here with me. Perhaps some day it may comfort you to tell me about your troubles: you don't know how often I thought of you and felt for you whilst you were away.'

Just then little Jane Hardiman, whose course of study had undergone temporary suspension on account of the extra bustle at home, came in for her hour's lesson. Sarah rose to go; but Mrs Grey begged her to sit down if she was not in a hurry, and wait till her niece was ready to walk home with her. Then business commenced.

The addition sum was produced, worked at last without one blunder; the blotted B elicited a mild rebuke; a flowerpot added to the sampler was inspected and approved. Next Jane, who had, in preparation, read it over by herself, was questioned on the parable of the lost sheep.[44]

'Where was the shepherd pasturing his flock?'

'In the wilderness.'

'What is a wilderness?'

'A barren place, without houses, or trees, or grass, or water.'

'But what then were the sheep to eat?'

Some moments spent in thought. 'Did they have manna, ma'am?'

'No, I do not suppose they had manna. In a wilderness there are certain spots where water springs out of the ground; and round about this water or fountain the ground is fertile, fruit-bearing and other shady trees grow, and grass springs up. I recollect once reading of a traveller who found a single most beautiful lily blooming by such a fountain. Doubtless the good shepherd fed his flock on a fruitful spot of the wilderness, as the Psalm says – 'He shall feed me in a green pasture, and lead me forth beside the waters of comfort'.[45] How many sheep were there?'

'A hundred.'

'Who took care of them?'

'Their shepherd.'

'Did the shepherd fall asleep at night and let the wolf come and catch them?'

'No.'

'No, certainly. He kept watch over his flock by night: if he saw a roaring lion or a great heavy bear coming to tear them, he rose and killed it or drove it away. Well, ninety-nine sheep followed him wherever he went: but what did one do?'

'It got away.'

'Where did it go?'

'Did it go into the other part of the wilderness?'

'Yes; quite away from the grass and water, where there was nothing but sand. It couldn't eat sand or drink sand, could it?'

'No, ma'am.'

'So it must have died very soon of hunger and thirst, even if no wild beast had devoured it. Did it die?'

'No; because the shepherd went and fetched it.'

'And when he found it, did he drive it before him, striking it and using angry words?'

'No; he laid it on his shoulders rejoicing, and all his neighbours rejoiced with him when it came safely back.'

'Very well. But this is not merely a beautiful tale about a shepherd and his flock; it is one of the sacred parables spoken by our blessed Saviour. What do I mean by a parable?' asked Mrs Grey.

A long pause: at last – 'Stories that tell about other things.'

'Really that will not do for an explanation,' said the teacher; 'because, though I understand what you mean, a person who knew nothing of what a parable is would be none the wiser. Perhaps your aunt will kindly help us.' Then, turning to her, 'Mrs Lane, will you inform your niece what a parable is?'

Sarah, who, as we know, had been well taught in her childhood, and who had greatly increased her religious knowledge during the years of her married life, replied readily, 'A spoken emblem; just as holly in a window tells us of Christmas.'

'Thank you, yes; or as the cross brings before our eyes Him who hung thereon. And since all our blessed Saviour's parables teach us something concerning God, or heaven, or our own duty, we must spare no pains to understand them. Now then, Jane, tell me the hidden meaning of this parable of the lost sheep. The shepherd is?…'

'Jesus Christ, who calls Himself the Good Shepherd.'[46]

'The flock are ?…'

'Everyone.'

'Not everyone. He has "other sheep".[47] The wilderness where they lived is this world. What was the fruitful spot where he pastured them?'

No answer. 'It is the Church,' continued Mrs Grey; 'the fold or pen if we speak under an emblem, the Church if we speak plainly. So this flock is not all people, but?…'

'Christian people.'

'Yes; in those days everyone who was a Christian at all belonged to the fold, or Church. What, then, did the sheep do who went wandering away?'

'It committed a sin.'

'And if the good shepherd had not gone to seek and to save that which was lost, what must have happened to it?'

'It must have died,' answered Jane, earnestly. 'But he went and looked about for it, and brought it back, and called all his friends and neighbours to rejoice with him.'

'Quite right. A verse which follows tells us who the friends and neighbours are: which verse is that?'

The child considered a moment, and then repeated, 'I say unto you, that likewise joy shall be in heaven over one sinner that repenteth, more than over ninety and nine just persons, which need no repentance'.[48]

'Or,' resumed the teacher, 'it is explained still more clearly at the end of the next parable: "Likewise, I say unto you, there is joy in the presence of the angels of God over one sinner that repenteth".'[49]

Now Mrs Grey, much as she loved Sarah Lane and admired her many good qualities, could not doubt that she fell into grievous error when she turned her back on the church of her baptism and followed ever so dear a person into schism; neither could she judge how eager the widow might be to lead her family after her. Therefore she added, trying not to look conscious –

'This sheep by sin wandered, as it is supposed, quite away from its kind shepherd's eye and care; but if, instead of going far, it had just crept through the paling and sat down outside the fold, and when its master called it back, had answered, "Master, I will follow thee whithersoever thou goest: but the grass outside the fold is more nourishing than that which grows inside, and the sheep whom I lived with there do not love and follow thee as entirely as I wish to do" – would its master have been pleased with it?'

'Oh no!'

'Yet this, Jane, is just what many people do now. They fancy they can find better food for their souls out of the Church than in it, and so join the dissenters; refusing to return, though they see written in the Bible that God added to the Church daily such as should be saved. That will do for the present: next time we will talk about the parable of the lost piece of money.'

Then Jane drew from her basket a large bunch of rose-coloured seaweed, the dock-leaved fucus, neatly smoothed on white cardboard, and said timidly, 'Please, ma'am, father desires his respects; and will you accept this, as you seem to fancy such things? It came up in the net last week, and he says he never found such a handsome piece of the sort before.'

Mrs Grey looked delighted: 'Oh, how lovely! I have nothing like it. Do thank your father very much for his kind present, and tell him it will be the beauty of my collection.'

So day by day Sarah Lane went to the Croft; and when it was not convenient for her to sit with Mrs Grey, took her needlework up into the nursery: for nurse, as her mistress knew, was a good steady person, much more likely to lead the young widow right than to be led wrong by her. Or sometimes she carried her work home, because Emma complained of being left always alone. Or sometimes, if the day was fine, and the material one that could not fade, she sat amongst the Pier Rocks sewing, much as she had sat years ago watching for her father's boat.

Native air, bracing sea breezes, a mind at rest as to the supply of daily bread – under the influence of these blessings her health rallied, her wasted figure became plumper, and her step more elastic. By little and little, old friends warmed towards her, and old customers came back; soon she had as many orders as she could execute.

Mrs Grey remarked, 'Why Sarah, you're growing quite stout and rosy: I do believe, after all, you may get as strong and live as long as any of us.'

The widow turned a little pale, but answered cheerfully, 'Please God, ma'am, I shall, if it is His will.' Only the cough continued, hack, hack, and scarcely seemed to get better.

One day the curate's wife came into her nursery, carrying a basin full of whitish jelly. 'Do try this for your cough, Mrs Lane,' said she; 'and if it does you good, I will tell you how to make some more.' Sarah tried it: the taste was rather pleasant, and in a day or two that extreme irritation at her chest abated. Then she learnt that this soothing jelly was made by boiling down a whitish seaweed (the carrageen, or Irish moss), which washes up in abundance on the Hastings coast, and adding a little sugar and lemon-juice to render it palatable.

Jane and Harry, when they walked on the shingle, used to fill their baskets with white weed for poor sick Aunt Sarah. Sometimes Harry got lazy, and would not take any pains to find the carrageen moss; but conscientious Jane looked carefully for it, and seldom failed to collect a little store, which was dried in the sun, and then laid by against cold wet weather, when she might not be able to go out seeking it. Her kind teacher had once made her learn the text, 'Whosoever shall give you a cup of water to drink in my name, because ye belong to Christ, verily I say unto you, he shall not lose his reward'; [50] explaining that any act of kindness done to any person for the sake of pleasing our Lord Jesus Christ will be remembered by Him and rewarded at the last day. This it was which made Jane so diligent; and often, when she felt inclined for a run in the lanes and green fields to gather hyacinths, or pink lychnis, or bunches of fiery poppies, she coaxed Harry to come down on the shingle instead, and look for pretty stones and shells and starfishes, whilst she picked up seaweed.

One certain Wednesday morning, symptoms of extraordinary bustle became evident in the snug cottage on the Tackle Way. To judge by appearances, a birth, marriage, or death at the least, must have been impending: no, it was only Emma Hardiman's quarterly cleaning-day which, having come round, occasioned such commotion. Frank was packed off from a quick breakfast to his fishing; Sarah received a broad hint that the sooner she vacated the sitting room the better it would be; Harry was sent into the garden with his knife and bits of wood; and Jane was bid 'put away her nonsense (a prize picture book received only the day previously for good conduct), and turn her hand to something useful'.

Now, as Emma on cleaning-days was fretted and snappish, Sarah pitied the poor child; so instead of starting for the Croft, she said to her sister-in-law, 'Indeed, I would rather not stir out today, or do needlework either; only that dress ought to go back at once to Ecclesbourne, as Mrs Bright said she wanted it in a hurry. Will you let the children carry it home for me? They can take their dinner with them, and keep out of our way all day, whilst I remain to help you. We shall get through the work twice as fast, and do it twice as well. Don't you remember the hand that I am at scrubbing and tidying?'

So the dress was neatly pinned up in a handkerchief for Jane to carry, and a basket stocked with two hunches of bread and two blocks of cold bacon was given to little Henry. Sarah sent also the bill, and showed Jane where to sign her name when she took the money; for Mrs Bright liked to pay at once for whatever she had.

It was a fine warm morning when the children started along the east cliff towards Ecclesbourne, trudging amongst all sorts of pleasant sights, sounds and smells. There was the scent of a hayfield, the sweetness of dog roses and honeysuckle, the fragrance of thyme beneath their feet; there were chirpings in the hedges, scattered skylarks in the air, a murmur of waves; there was blue sky above their heads, bright living green and golden sunshine around them, glittering sea far down below the cliff, flowers in the grass and about the hedges, butterflies here, there, and everywhere.

Cap in hand, shouting and jumping, away ran Harry after the butterflies; whilst elder Jane, precious parcel in hand, plodded steadily forward, sometimes calling her truant brother, sometimes waiting for him to come up with her. This walk over the glorious east hill was doubly delightful after those many strolls along the shingle.

Mrs Bright lived in a pretty house that stood in its own neat garden. The children felt quite shy as they opened the wicket-gate and proceeded soberly along the gravel walk up to the house door. Perhaps Mrs Bright would see them out of window, and wonder what they wanted. Harry got behind Jane, and looked as if he had never run in his life, much less after a butterfly; Jane put the best face she could on the matter, and rang the bell.

But when a maidservant, having opened the door and asked their business, showed them into the parlour, Mrs Bright's good-natured smile and manner gave them courage. She had spied them as they came along the garden – not treading on the borders or meddling with the flowers – and wondered in her own mind who that neat girl and boy might be. When she found they were Mrs Lane's niece and nephew come with her new dress, saw Jane write her name readily at the foot of the bill, and noticed her civil 'Thank you, ma'am' and curtsy, she was quite pleased, and showed them several pretty things. First of all, they watched a large white cockatoo crack a nut, and heard him say 'Pretty Poll', and 'Pretty cockatoo'; next they saw a glass bowl full of water, in which swam gold and silver fishes, much handsomer than those their father brought ashore in his boat. Mrs Bright showed them some coloured pictures – amongst which Jane recognised the good shepherd seeking his lost sheep – in a handsome old clasped Bible, and gave a story book to the girl, but shook her head when she heard the boy could not say his letters. Then, handing each of the children a cup of milk, which they drank at once, and a hunch of sweet cake to serve as pudding after their bread and bacon, she sent them away very well pleased.

Down the steep cliff steps they scrambled to the rocky beach below, to sit on a huge stone which was hollowed 'something' – as Harry said – 'like father's armchair' and eat their dinner. By this time the beauty of the day was gone; clouds which in the early morning had been ranged along the horizon were spread over a great portion of the sky, and the air felt much cooler. The children, however, were hungry and happy enough not to notice these changes, but held their feast with great glee. Then they had a long game at hide-and-seek in and out amongst the rocky fragments, Jane hunting for Harry, and tickling him well when she found him. At last she proposed setting off homewards; but Harry by this time was tired and sleepy, so she sat down in the 'armchair' with his curly head in her lap, and soon both the little ones were fast asleep.

When Jane woke, it was with a start and a loud sound roaring in her ears. She felt chilled and cramped, but could not at first remember where she was; when she did remember, she shook up Harry in a great fright, and bade him keep fast hold of her hand and come straight back to the cliff path. During their sleep a thick brown fog had risen from the ground like smoke; it hid the cliff, and even the rocks and shingle at a very few yards' distance: only Jane could make out the sea distinctly, because the tide was rising; waves were foaming, breaking, roaring, close at hand amongst the huge stones; not a moment must be lost in escaping for their lives.

They scrambled as fast as they could from the terrible advancing sea; but that was slowly, for the fog thickened and thickened, and many a fall they got slipping on the slimy tangle. Hand in hand they kept on stoutly, but in the darkness turned to one side, being quite unable to make out the cliff. Suddenly a shower of foam fell on them. Harry stood stock-still, hiding his face against his sister and trembling all over; he did not cry or utter a word, but he could not move one step further. 'Come on, dear,' said Jane, trying not to seem frightened; 'perhaps we shall see the steps directly.' But Harry could not stir; he clung to his sister, utterly unable to move a foot forward. Louder and louder the tumult, thicker and thicker the foam, closer and closer came the strong, broken, irresistible sweep of sea.

Jane felt ready to sit down and cry; but she remembered the Good Shepherd seeking His lost sheep, and in her heart prayed Him now to seek and save His little lambs. Next – there was no help for it – she caught up Harry in her arms, and stumbled as well as she could guess towards the cliff.

At last they dimly discerned it, not so high as at the spot where they descended, stretching sheer, rugged, upwards; but no trace of steps was on its precipitous face. This was a different point of the east hill, and at high tide the sea dashed against its foot.

A little above the ground a narrow shelf jutted out of the rock. This they succeeded in gaining, but further ascent was impossible. Jane made Harry kneel by her side, and together they repeated the Lord's Prayer in small, sad voices: then, sitting down, she took her brother on her lap and, rocking backwards and forwards, tried to sing him to sleep before the dreadful death came; praying in her heart all the while as well as she was able; not even starting, lest she should wake the little one, when the first cold touch of water reached her feet.

But it was not God's will that the water flood should drown them, and the deep swallow them up; at that very moment lights flashed above their heads, and loud shouts reached them. Jane screamed in answer, bidding Harry scream too, lest they should not be heard; and scream he did with all his might. Then a man secured to a stout rope was swung over the cliff by his companions, and took both children in his strong arms; then all three were drawn up into safety, just as a foaming wave swept over the rocky shelf.

'O that men would therefore praise the Lord for His goodness, and declare the wonders that He doeth for the children of men!'[51]

Next Sunday morning –

'Frank Hardiman and his family desire to return thanks to Almighty God for great mercies received,' gave out Mr Grey, before reading the 'General Thanksgiving' – at which announcement half the congregation turned their heads in one direction.

There knelt Frank, his handsome, sunburnt face full of emotion: on his right hand was Emma, on his left Jane, holding Harry almost as tightly as when they clung together on the terrible rock. But who could that be with bowed head, kneeling next to the boy, and sobbing in her prayers? There was no mistaking the close widow's bonnet and heavy black dress, though the patient widowed face remained hidden; once more Sarah Lane was kneeling where so often she had knelt by her father's side: if that day her sweet voice could not be heard joining in the hymns, doubtless in her heart she praised God.

Jane had said, 'Please do come, Aunt Sarah' – so she yielded to one longing of her divided heart, and worshipped once more in the familiar holy house; yet the next Sunday found her again amongst the Methodists. 'John,' she pleaded, 'seemed upbraiding me all through the service for deserting him in his cold grave.'

'Oh, Mrs Grey,' she said, earnestly, 'he may have been right or wrong, I can't tell; but it's not for me to sit in judgement on him who loved Christ and spent himself to save souls. I led him into sin, but he led me to repentance: if I'm patient, he showed me first the way; and if I'm humble, he prayed without ceasing that I might become so.'

'God forbid,' replied Mrs Grey, tenderly, 'that either you or myself should sit in judgement on any man, least of all on one who loved our blessed Lord, and laboured to do Him service. This I know,' – and the wife coloured – 'your husband taught my husband a living lesson of boldness, self-denial, and trampling false shame under foot. Often, when I see him earnest in the pulpit, or zealous in his schools, or energetic amongst his poor, I remember John Lane, and thank God for his example. Do not let us dwell on the worn, suffering body, at rest now in its dust; let us lift our minds towards the free soul, resting, we both hope, in Paradise. Oh, dear Sarah, if he now sees that there was a more excellent way than he himself trod, can you imagine he would grudge you the knowledge of it? Would he not rather say, "Be very jealous for the unity of Christ's fold, even whilst you open a wide heart of love to all who love the Lord Jesus?" It is not my part to exhort you; only recollect, if ever you allow my husband to teach you anything which you need to learn, he will but be repaying to you some part of all he owes John Lane.'

From that day forward one great barrier between the widow and the Church was removed: she no longer fancied that Church people were criticising and branding her dead John; she no longer felt as if, by continuing a Methodist, she stood by one whose excellences were unappreciated and whose errors, if such she admitted them to have been, were triumphantly condemned. Often before this, when she sat at work listening to the earnest, simple words in which Mrs Grey expounded parable or miracle to Jane, and drew out its lesson of mercy or warning – sometimes dwelling on the holiness without which no man shall see the Lord, sometimes on the yearning divine compassion which sought and saved that which was lost, sometimes on the many mansions, sometimes on the one fold under one Shepherd – conscience had spoken; now at length she listened to its voice only to answer, 'Speak, Lord, for Thy servant heareth.'[52]

'Line upon line, precept upon precept; here a little, and there a little' – so the message was revealed to her as she was able to receive it. First she opened to her tried friend the curate's wife, stating her difficulties, willing, if it might be, to have them removed; next she took courage, spoke to Mr Grey himself, and found in him a patient listener, a faithful guide, and one who felt and professed deep obligation to John Lane.

Back from meeting house to church, through church up to the blessed Sacrament of the Altar, the grace of God led her.

Another five years of patient progress passed away; let us take a parting glance at Sarah Lane.

Sarah Lane still? Yes, though faithful John Archer tried once and again to win a kind answer. She continues to wear black for her dear husband's sake, and at least once in the year journeys up to London to see and tend his grave. Though she cannot preach on the highways, his example stirs her up to energy in the Sunday school, and tenderness in visiting sufferers. Many a time has she stinted her own meal to feed the hungry; many a time has she curtailed her night's rest to nurse the sick. She teaches Jane her business, calls her 'her right hand' and 'little forewoman', yet feels perhaps a secret preference for Harry, so like his grandfather.

Though very diligent at her work, and frequently in the season hurried by her employers, she is seldom absent from the Wednesday and Friday morning service, held alternately at St Clement's and All Saints' Churches. Sunday she strictly and thankfully observes; partaking, whenever an opportunity offers, of the comfortable Sacrament of Christ's Body and Blood.

Certainly now neither the prettiest nor the merriest woman in Hastings, but I truly believe this widow is one of the happiest: having chosen that good part which shall not be taken from her; thankful that her idol was removed for a season, if so she might receive him for ever; able to say at last, 'Whom have I in heaven but Thee? and there is none upon earth that I desire in comparison of Thee. Amen. Even so, come, Lord Jesus.'[53]

NOTES

1. Railway guides written by George Bradshaw (1801–53) were a national institution by the latter half of the nineteenth century. The point here, presumably, is that Brompton-on-Sea is an out-of-the-way place.

2. Mrs Grundy, an imaginary character typifying conventional opinion and society's judgements, derives from Thomas Morton's play *Speed the Plough* (1798).

3. 'If it's not true, it's well devised' (Italian).

4. William Hone (1780–1842), English journalist, bookseller, publisher, and satirist.

5. *Realmah* was written by Sir Arthur Helps (1813–75), a valued adviser to Queen Victoria.

6. Tomato.

7. Boreas was the ancient Greek god of the north wind who lived in Thrace.

8. Possibly a reference to the nursery rhyme quoted in Gaskell's *Mary Barton*, chapter 38: 'Clap hands, Daddy comes / With his pocket full of plums / And a cake for Johnny'.

9. 'What you like does you good' (Italian).

10. 'Complexion' (Italian).

11. 'Hurrah!' (Italian).

12. 'Blue rock thrush' (Italian). Rossetti incorrectly places the adjective before the noun.

13. 'My friend' (Italian).

14. Another expression for loaded dice.

15. 'House' (Italian).

16. Benvenuto Cellini (1500–71), sculptor, goldsmith, author, soldier and celebrated figure of the Italian Renaissance.

17. Giorgione (1477–1510), Italian painter of the Venetian school.

18. Tintoretto (1518–94), Venetian painter.

19. 'Gentlemen' (Italian).

20. The Italian for 'Titian'.

21. Tintoretto's actual name ('Tintoretto' was a nickname derived from his father's profession of dyer – 'tintore').

22. Lupo Vorace literally means 'Greedy Wolf'.

23. In order to appease the gods, Andromeda's father chained her to a rock to be sacrificed to a dragon. However, she was rescued by Perseus, who killed the dragon and married her.

24. '*Vascitammò*' is not identifiable with any town or village near Naples. The narrator might be misunderstanding the phrase '*Facite a mo*', literally meaning 'hurry up', which the Neapolitans may be saying to her in jest.

25. 'For the two of us and for the little ones' (Italian).

26. 'Some macaroni pasta' (Italian).

27. 'Small squid' (Neapolitan).

28. Felice and Gioconda both mean 'happy' in Italian; Felice Maria is the name of the little boy, Maria Gioconda that of the little girl.

29. The word signifies both 'country' and 'town' (Italian).

30. 'And what's the danger? There are no crocodiles, are there?' (Italian).

31. 'Our Lord' (Italian).

32. 'Truly marvellous' (Italian).

33. 'Not too bad, both of them' (Italian).

34. 'You descend from the stars, O King of heaven, / Into a cold and frosty cave: / O divine Child / I will always love you! / O blessed Lord / How dearly You paid for loving me!' (Italian).

35. 'They have no father' (Italian).

36. 'Yes, Mummy' (Italian).

37. 'Our Lord will look after them' (Italian).

38. 'They're only children – poor children, my dear poor children' (Italian).

39. 'Vanna, my dear Vanna! Where are you? Answer me… answer me, my dear children' (Italian).

40. 'O Lord, O Lord, have pity on us' (Italian).

41. 'Yes, my dear Vanna, we are going back; God forbid that I should lose you too' (Italian).

42. 'Our Lord is good, and I'm sure He will have made them blessed' (Italian).

43. 'Dives in hell': see Luke 16: 19–31. 'Dives' is the Latin Vulgate's translation for 'rich man'.

44. Luke 15: 4.

45. Psalms 23: 1, 2.

46. John 10: 11.

47. John 10: 16.

48. Luke 15: 7.

49. Luke 15: 10.

50. Mark 9: 41.

51. Psalms 107: 8.

52. 1 Samuel 3: 9.

53. For the first part of the quotation, see Psalms 73: 25.

Christina Georgina Rossetti was born in London on 5th December 1830 to the Italian poet Gabriele Rossetti and Frances Polidori Rossetti, who brought up Christina and her siblings as devout evangelical Anglicans. This strong religious influence would shape much of her life and work, as would her father's enthusiasm for literature – all the Rossetti children became writers. Her brothers, Dante Gabriel and William Michael, were founder members of the Pre-Raphaelite Brotherhood, and Dante Gabriel also found fame as a painter, occasionally using his sister as a model for his paintings.

Christina Rossetti's first verses were published in 1847 by her grandfather. In 1850, she contributed seven poems to the short-lived Pre-Raphaelite journal *The Germ*. After her father was forced into retirement by the loss of his eyesight, Christina helped her mother run a school to help the family's finances, but it was not a success, and it lasted only a year. Although Christina lived with her mother for almost all her life, she mixed with celebrated figures such as Whistler, Swinburne and the Reverend Charles Dodgson (author of *Alice's Adventures in Wonderland* under the pseudonym of Lewis Carroll), who were friends of her brothers. She never married, rejecting two offers for religious reasons, even though this caused her grief. Her religiosity was such that she could only enjoy Swinburne's *Atalanta in Calydon* after sticking strips of paper over the parts of the poem she considered anti-religious. In 1862, her most famous work, *Goblin Market and other Poems*, was published, securing her place among Victorian poets. It was followed by further poetry, a book of nursery rhymes for children, a prose fiction work, *Commonplace* (1870), and works on religion. In the 1870s she worked for the Society for Promoting Christian Knowledge, although in this time Dante Gabriel suffered a breakdown which affected his sister deeply, and she suffered from declining physical health. After Dante Gabriel's death in 1882, Christina lived quietly, devoting herself to religion. She died in London on 29th December 1894.

Rossetti's predominant themes were unhappy love, death, premature resignation, and the renunciation of earthly desire. She was considered as a successor to Alfred Tennyson as Poet Laureate, though not chosen, and her poem 'In the Bleak Midwinter' is still known as a popular Christmas carol.

HESPERUS PRESS CLASSICS

Hesperus Press, as suggested by the Latin motto, is committed to bringing near what is far – far both in space and time. Works written by the greatest authors, and unjustly neglected or simply little known in the English-speaking world, are made accessible through new translations and a completely fresh editorial approach. Through these classic works, the reader is introduced to the greatest writers from all times and all cultures.

For more information on Hesperus Press, please visit our website: **www.hesperuspress.com**

ET REMOTISSIMA PROPE

SELECTED TITLES FROM HESPERUS PRESS

Author	Title	Foreword writer
Jane Austen	*Love and Friendship*	Fay Weldon
Aphra Behn	*The Lover's Watch*	
Charlotte Brontë	*The Green Dwarf*	Libby Purves
Emily Brontë	*Poems of Solitude*	Helen Dunmore
Anton Chekhov	*Three Years*	William Fiennes
Wilkie Collins	*Who Killed Zebedee?*	Martin Jarvis
William Congreve	*Incognita*	Peter Ackroyd
Joseph Conrad	*The Return*	Colm Tóibín
Charles Dickens	*The Haunted House*	Peter Ackroyd
Fyodor Dostoevsky	*The Double*	Jeremy Dyson
George Eliot	*Amos Barton*	Matthew Sweet
Henry Fielding	*Jonathan Wild the Great*	Peter Ackroyd
F. Scott Fitzgerald	*The Rich Boy*	John Updike
E.M. Forster	*Arctic Summer*	Anita Desai
Elizabeth Gaskell	*Lois the Witch*	Jenny Uglow
Thomas Hardy	*Fellow-Townsmen*	Emma Tennant
L.P. Hartley	*Simonetta Perkins*	Margaret Drabble
Nathaniel Hawthorne	*Rappaccini's Daughter*	Simon Schama
John Keats	*Fugitive Poems*	Andrew Motion
D.H. Lawrence	*Daughters of the Vicar*	Anita Desai
Katherine Mansfield	*In a German Pension*	Linda Grant
Prosper Mérimée	*Carmen*	Philip Pullman
Sándor Petőfi	*John the Valiant*	George Szirtes
Alexander Pope	*The Rape of the Lock*	Peter Ackroyd
Robert Louis Stevenson	*Dr Jekyll and Mr Hyde*	Helen Dunmore
Leo Tolstoy	*Hadji Murat*	Colm Tóibín
Mark Twain	*Tom Sawyer, Detective*	
Oscar Wilde	*The Portrait of Mr W.H.*	Peter Ackroyd
Virginia Woolf	*Carlyle's House and Other Sketches*	Doris Lessing